Spectrum

Royal Palm Beach Writers

**The Writing Group
of
Royal Palm Beach, Florida**

is proud to present this book

to the reading public.

ENJOY!

Spectrum

Ingenious Publishers Inc.
Short Stories, Essays, Poems, Fiction, Non-fiction

Royal Palm Beach Writers
www.RoyalPalmBeachWriters.com

ISBN-978-1-7329696-1-2
Printed in the United States of America

Cataloging-in-Publication data for this book is available from the Library of Congress .

Cover Design by: Virginia Guido and Karina Felix
Cover Artwork/Illustration by: Karina G. Felix

 Published by: Ingenious Publishers Inc.
www.IngeniousPublishers.com

The paper used in this publication meets the minimum requirements of the American National Standards for information Sciences – Permanence of Paper for Printed Library Material.

Dedication

This volume of literary offerings is dedicated to all writers,
would-be writers, and readers who have a passion
for the written word.

Acknowledgments

We extend our heartfelt appreciation to
Virginia Guido and Karina Felix
for their invaluable dedication and care in the
preparation of this issue of **Spectrum** - Volume 15.

Spectrum is a collection of original writing
from members of **Royal Palm Beach Writers**:
The Writing Group of Royal Palm Beach, Florida.

The **stories, essays,** and **poems** in this anthology are extensions of personal imagination, with some of the pieces derived from monthly writing prompts. Thus, a few segments might have similar titles or themes. In those instances, we hope you'll enjoy reading these like-minded elements of creativity, dreams, and fantasies.

Table of Contents

Hartley Barnes

Love Dilemma 3

In My Backyard, Waiting for My Cake 37

Birth Control Glasses 71

Man on the Street 125

Sugar 171

The Trumpet Blows 191

Margie Bonner

A Glimpse into a Lady's Life 39

An Unusual Arrival 121

Don Conway

Muley Bates... 7

The Ugly Girl and the Beautiful Woman.................... 61

Prissy.. 87

Harry, the Horse.. 151

Economics 101... 197

Karina G. Felix

It Found You 35

Not My Fight 81

I Cried for Us 135

The Dance I Danced 177

I'd Rather Die 195

Gloria Ferrara

Tommy 27

My Best Friend 67

A Joyful Noise 213

Virginia Guido

Street Life 11

Running with the Devil 43

A New York State of Mind 93

Unforgettable 137

Isn't She Lovely? 179

Pink Lemonade 205

Betty Jean Kult

Never Go Hungry 15

Olivia the Ostrich 65

The Teacup 165

Just a Smile 203

Shelley Leiman

Writers' Block 1

My Shoes 31

Post-Apocalyptic Return of the Olfactory System 75

The Hat 109

Minnie Bottoms 185

Confession of an age Junkie 169

Daddy 211

Dorothy Littlefield

The New Car 101

Judith Ann Pelio

War Is Hell 17

25 Hour Day Surgery 55

Life With My Fur Babies 113

John Rifenberg

Her Feet in the Sand 19

The Weather 79

Cross Roads 141

No Siren? No Lights? 173

It's Only a Piece of Metal 193

Virginia (Ginny) Smythe

I Want to Dance 23

Grandma and the Machine 49

Here and Now 97

Inheritance 169

You Left Us too Soon 189

Patti Thomas

Born to Cheer, Not to Run 45

Flying Backwards 157

Tajuana Troy

Invisible Woman 29

Destiny 91

This is 40 145

Heart Beat 183

Scribbles 209

Shanda N. Whittle

Rock Chronicles I: Family Reunion 105

Rock Chronicles II: The End 215

Royal Palm Beach Writers

Authors 221

Programs and Events 226

WRITER'S BLOCK
Shelley Leiman

Please don't put me on. You know as well as I do my suffering has been unbearable; the piercing headaches, sleepless nights, poor appetite, my face and spirit gaunt. And now the trembling hands. Oh yes, I know you've been there too…you hibernated in your room, locked the door, issued alternate sobs and profanity. But you recovered and sheepishly returned to the real world, grinning with a strange sense of pride, waving that first draft in your hand. And now you expect me to somehow magically recover from my malaise and share your joy. It doesn't work that way. My thoughts are constantly drawn to the recent loss of a very dear, significant person in my life, a loss I have not been able to reconcile. I am in mourning. I've taken long walks to clear my mind, grasped at straws to find a viable means of generating a semblance of thoughts that would appeal to me as an author or you as a reader. My mind has flitted from interesting characters to interpretations of dreams that are a side effect of medication, dreams I hesitate to share. My thoughts are drawn to memories of the past. Is this because I am uncertain of the future? I've never considered therapy before, but it is my inability to write that necessitates my search for help. You've been there and recovered, so give me time to be inspired and whole again.

LOVE DILEMMA
Hartley Barnes

Walking off and not looking back took all the strength Chess had. Leaving behind what he cherished most. Gwen watched him walked away. He turned the first corner and launched into a sprint. Tears rushed from his eyes like raindrops blowing in the wind. Gwen's face appeared in front of him, distorted from her pain. He thought he heard her say, "Turn around Chess!" He yelled, "No! Tomorrow is a new day. Make the best of it, you will understand in time." He continued to run, not knowing where he was going, then he slowed to a walk.

Chess met Gwen on a warm gusty June afternoon five years earlier. She was wearing purple shorts and a matching tank top, her favorite color. Her wig blew off her head and landed on his face.

"Oh, my God!" She said with a bittersweet smile. "I am so, so sorry."

"I think it looks better on you," he said, laughingly, feeling a little embarrassed for her. He tried to take some of the stings of the moment away. "You don't need to wear a wig. My name is Chess."

She responded, "It's a girl thing, you know. I'm Gwen."

That afternoon they saw butterflies and the beginning of a relationship that changed the dynamics of their lives. They reinvented each other. Gwen was a joy to be with;

she personified woman. As the relationship progressed, He learned so many beautiful things about her, especially her delightful idiosyncrasies. If she sang in the shower, it was an invitation for him to join her and he had better have a good excuse if he did not. The only song she sang was "Singin´ in the Rain," and of course, he had to join her so they could be a duet.

At the dinner table, Gwen insisted they nibble from each other's plates, and that Chess have the last bite from hers. Her reasoning was she would never let Chess go hungry. If he had been away from her more than a day, on his return, excitement gushed from her like a dragster racing down a track. Her smile was so captivating it did not allow Chess to be sad. Regardless of how he was feeling, it put him in a bucket of Maraschino cherries and vanilla ice cream. Living with Gwen was a honeymoon without the marriage and education of how to love and be loved.

She cherished the small things, like when he patted her on the butt when saying hello and holding her hand while driving or rocking on a seesaw. They were dangerously in love, and then Chess went to see the doctor.

The information Chess gave the doctor along with the results of tests confirmed the doctor's suspicions. Once again, Chess life was going to change. Is happiness a signal tragedy is going to strike? Is contentment a prelude to a sinkhole that devours two people and turns their tranquility into hell? He had to do some soul searching. How could he protect Gwen, and save her from his demise? He agonized over his choices and avoided her questions. Gwen knew something changed, Chess demeanor altered as had Gwen's.

Chess was so absorbed in wanting to protect her. He ignored her calling to him. He wished she were never in his life. He dreaded exposing her to what would come. Love had him in a dilemma. He had to choose between the lesser of two evils; either way, they lose.

"Was I selfish for not wanting Gwen to see me deteriorate? My pillow wet many nights while she slept. God, Gwen deserves to be happy, why Lord? Is there a lesson? Give her a break and make me whole again."

Time became more precious. The physical pain was bearable, but the mental anguish had Chess's heart in a clutch on the road to darkness. He labored over the finale of their series. He decided to leave, then had second thoughts.

He wanted her to remember him like the healthy man she met and not the vegetable that he would become. "Telling her what is wrong will devastate and rip her apart, and it will be my fault." Is it fair to her? He repeatedly asked himself. "Can I stand on my own?" The thought kept going through his head like a shooting star and vanishing without an answer.

He walked and walked and ending back the next morning to find Gwen sitting at their front door; her eyes were red and swollen. She saw him and screamed, "Why did you leave me?" She leaped into his arms while squeezing the breath out of him. "Why did you leave me?"

At that moment, he realized the only choice he had was to stay by her side as he made the journey to the other side.

"Gwen, I have brain cancer."

"Chess, I have breast cancer."

MULEY BATES
Don Conway

Author's note: This is one of a series of stories called Movie Minor Characters in which I develop a fictional history of a minor character in a popular movie. Muley Bates is such a person in the movie "The Grapes of Wrath," based on author John Steinbeck's 1939 master-piece novel of the same name. (Note: In the book, Muley Bates is named Muley Graves.)

It's 1932. It was just getting on to dusk when Tom Joad and Preacher Casy approached the Joad farmstead in central Oklahoma. Just released from prison, Tom had hoped to find Ma and the rest of the family at the cabin. What they found instead was Muley Bates. Muley was slightly "tetched in the head." Ma Joad said Muley was slow.

When Tom and Preacher Casy found the cabin empty, they speculated on what had become of the Joad family. It wasn't until Muley Bates approached them from a dried-up cotton field that they got the full story.

"Gone," Said Muley. "Gone. Just like all the other families in the county. Goin' to California to look for work.

"Gone just like my wife Helen and our three kids is gone. But not me! I ain't a goin.' No sir! I ain't a goin.' Two years in a row, my crops failed. So, I couldn't pay the rent. How could I pay the rent when I didn't have so much as a penny of cash money? I couldn't even get enough credit at the store to feed all of us. We ate rabbits and even a rattlesnake we was so desperate for food. Finally, Helen sez, 'I can't take this no more Muley. I'm not gonna stay here and watch these children starve to death.' So she and the kids took a ride with the Askew family and went off to California. But not me! No sir, I ain't a leavin.'

"A course folks say I'm tetched in the head. Do you think I'm tetched?" He asked Tom and the preacher. "Well, maybe, I am. But my Paw got this land in the Rush of '89, and I was born on it in '95. Worked it all our lives when cotton and wheat was king. Why I went to that little schoolhouse just down the road. Every Sunday we cleaned up and went to the church meeting house. We even saw you preach there 'couple of times, Preacher. Same's true of Helen. She was born on this land just like I was. We went to school together and grew up side by side—her family and my family. Things was good then. A man could keep a roof over his head, feed his family, and have a few dollars left over at the end of the growin' season. We was poor, sure enough, but we had family, and church, and honest work to do. Couldn't ask for much more for folks like us.

"In '28, the rains stopped a comin.' In '31, the winds started to blowin' and it just blowed this poor land away. Can't grow nuthin' now. Then the landlords and the banks and the sheriff started comin.' They was worse than the dust storms. 'Can't pay up? Then git off the land,' they said. Just as if being born here and workin' here all your life didn't mean nothing. That's what we was to them—nothin.'

"A course, folks started leavin.' Okies! That's what they call us. Just damn poor ole' Okies. Did I tell ya Helen and the children left? Up 'n gone to California.

"As for your family Tom well, they held out as long as they could. Cause of your Grandpa and Grandma I reckon. They all went over to your Uncle John's place just a few days ago. They're gettin' ready to leave, too, seems to me. But I'm stayin.' I just move from place to place so the sheriff don't catch me. I hit him over the head with a stick one night so he don't come out into the fields lookin' for me no more. I tell myself I'm looking after these farms until the families come back. But I know they ain't nobody comin' back. So I guess I'm just an ole ghost wanderin' from farm to farm. But I ain't a leavin.' No sir, I ain't a leavin.'"

"Well what are you gonna do now, Tom?" the preacher asked.

"It's gettin' late now," Tom said. "Reckon' I'll stay here for tonight and go on over to Uncle John's place in the morning. See if I can catch up with Ma and the rest. Why don't you come along with me, Preacher?"

The next morning, Tom and Preacher Casy left Muley Bates on the abandoned farm. They went to Uncle John's place, reunited with the family and, along with the preacher, set off for California in director John Ford's classic 1940 movie "The Grapes of Wrath."

STREET LIFE
Virginia Guido

Dear Cousin Maria,

I'm so glad that you and your brother, Stephen, are finally coming to visit us! However, I understand that my husband has given you directions to the house, including his famous "short cuts." Do not, I reiterate, do not take his short cuts. They will lead you to a gravel road that takes you across the tracks of an abandoned railroad. So, unless you own an all-terrain vehicle or possess heavy-duty shocks on your car, I suggest you ignore his guidelines. Otherwise, you will need new tires and dental work from the wild ride you will experience!

Hence, I feel obligated to give you a heads up about a more efficient route to our home. Due to recent construction (Yes, once again they are paving my paradise to put up another parking lot.), your GPS may not give you the correct directions. Here is the quickest, non-threatening way to our place:

From your house, travel north to the Korean War Veterans' Memorial Parkway (You know, the old Richmond Parkway, by which its new name is longer than the road itself).

Exit the KWVMP at the Richmond Avenue exit and turn right at the Stop N Shop (Although it may now be a King Kullen. Last year, it was a Pathmark Supermarket! Ah, this economy!).

Continue along Richmond Avenue for three blocks towards the fire-engine red house on your left (It is not really a firehouse; someone actually painted the house that color. You can't miss it!).

Travel two more blocks past that house (The house had no bearing on your journey; I just wanted you to see the house so you can understand that there is no accounting for taste in my neighborhood.)

Make a left on Richmond Road and go four blocks to the traffic light on Richmond Terrace; wait for the light to turn green and make a quick right turn on Richmond Loop (If you turn left, you will find yourself crashing into someone's house, because this is a three-way, not four-way intersection).

My house is the sixth house on the left, from the corner, number 64. It is butterscotch with pale blue shutters. These are not the colors that I originally chose, but I did tell my husband that I wanted a yellow and blue home, forgetting that he's colorblind!

When you get to our humble abode, go straight up the driveway, past the giant yew trees (planted for privacy, thank you, Nosy Rosy, the scourge of our community) to our backyard.

One more thing, our dog is huge but sociable. He's so friendly that he'll show you where we keep our valuables if you rub his belly. Just beware of the militant squirrel who insists on throwing his half-eaten nuts at us every time we barbeque. Bring an umbrella for protection.

Again, I'm looking forward to seeing you next Saturday, May the fourth (be with you?) at two o'clock. Have a safe trip.

-Virginia

13

NEVER GO HUNGRY

Betty Jean Kult

I went to the market on Monday
Just to purchase a couple of things
But the moment I entered the store
My appetite took wings
Everything looked so appealing
My appetite was reeling even the
Kumquats and the artichokes began
To look good for eating
I picked up some fresh veggies
Thinking I'd make a steamy pot of soup
It will taste so good after the snow I scoop
Next, I couldn't resist some cookies
A pie and a chocolate cake, I have a busy
week ahead, no time to bake
After a while, it didn't matter how much I spent
If it looked good to me, into my cart, it went
Oh no! Miss Prissy Miss I can't let her see me like this
Here I am in old sweats and not a trace of makeup on my
face
She is all dressed up and looks so pretty with every
hair in place.
So quickly I try this strategy because I don't think she has
seen me
I pull up my hoodie over my hair and my sunglasses I
start to wear
She passes, and I let out a sigh, I guess with my clev-

er disguise I got by
Then a voice from behind says, "Sally, is that you?"
    I stop for a minute then I just keep on walking
If I turn around that blabbermouth will never stop talking
So I hurry to the checkout thank goodness I quickly get through
I have to get home. I have a lot to do
    Finally, I'm home, and I'm unpacking my meals and treats
As soon as I finish, I will pickle my beets
Now, where did I put them and the other things I went for?
Oh no! I forgot to buy them, but I'm not going back to the store

WAR IS HELL
Judith Ann Pelio

I'm on the battlefield right now,
 They say that you're the foe,
My head is pounding with the sounds
 Of words that hurt me so.

They say that I must bury you,
 That you're my enemy,
But something in my heart believes
 That you would not hurt me.

They say your gun is aimed at me,
 You're mean, and you will kill,
And though I've heard you say you'll shoot,
 I can't believe you will.

But yet my eyes have seen you there
 Just standing at my feet,
Plus, I have seen your gun in hand
 Until I would retreat!

I hear the shots of words explode,
 Each one is aimed at me,
And even though you hold the gun,
 Your wrong I still can't see.

For I have lived there by your side
 And I was born to you,

But now I'm told to disbelieve
  Those 'truths' you swore were true.

Confusion fills my inner thoughts
  And settles in my heart,
They say it was your bullets mom
  That tore me all apart!

And now I'm covered in my blood,
  My pain is agony,
And still, I look to blame myself
  For what you did to me.

This battle, you keep telling me,
  Would end if I'd stay still,
If I'd give in without a fight,
  In silence, do your will.

So, through my pain, I did just that,
  Hoping it would end,
But when you finished, you began
  To do it all again.

And so, it goes, day in day out,
  The hell that no one saw.
It then became my way of life
  Since you had won the war.

HER FEET IN THE SAND
John F. Rifenberg

The sun started to creep over the calm morning ocean. The pink, orange, and yellow colors came first with blades of rays stabbing through the predawn sky. The sun was making its grand entrance. She rubbed her toes in the cool sand, thinking,

Nothing is better than this. The smell of the beach, on a new morning, Mother Nature is the greatest artist of all. The warm sun makes this an extraordinary day.

She had her hair done the day before, colored and highlighted. That was a first, just another dream until today. Now, a new problem: having to worry about a windy morning at the beach, and messing her new hair-style. Her hands felt her new dress, loving its feel; it was soft cotton, cream in color with her favorite flowers in her hair, white lilies.

It was as if she had new skin on a new body. No more bruises, no more fighting for her life and her children's lives. No more insane loud screaming. She marveled at her body; through it all, she had no broken bones. To forget the past and now look to the future was her mind-set.

A voice broke the spell. "Where do you want me to set-up the music?"

Both of them had made the playlist. They each liked the power –ballads of the '80s. Then add a little Ed

Sheeran, with his songs of love. She had always loved music even though she couldn't sing a lick. Now she sang every morning. Especially this morning; all of them will be special now that love was in the air.

Once the sun rose, warmth filled the air. She knew they'd have to start soon, but the pastor was late. Brunch was planned, the Bloody Marys were ordered. The sand started to feel warm on her toes. She loved the beach.

In the distance, she envisioned a man on a white horse. He looked like a prince. He rode directly in front of her and smiled as he dismounted from the horse, his blue eyes matching the sky, "I'm here to save you and love you."

This would have been really romantic, but instead, her prince drove up to the beach in his old classic convertible. Most of her life, she was just glad to have a car that had gas and wasn't one day away from being repossessed. Seagulls flew over them as music filled the air. It was time to start, but the pastor hadn't arrived. Then, they heard the honking of a car horn.

Everyone got to see the pastor run thru the parking lot and fall into the sand, tripping over his own feet. "Don't start without me!"

He laughed at himself as he dusted off the sand.

What he didn't know, is that she would have had the lifeguard read the vows, if need be. She was getting married this morning.

As her best friend played her favorite song "Stairway to Heaven," she glided down a homemade path in the beach. She felt her toes in the warm sand and smiled to herself. This is where they met, on the beach, when she learned to trust again. They fell for each other in that second, love at first sight!

She looked up and saw him totally focused on her as if she were the only woman in the world. She watched his face light up as she came closer. His happiness reflected in his smile and eyes. There would never be fear, worry, or pain with this man. Just then, the sea breeze came blowing ashore.

She thought, "My hair! …Oh, the hell with it!"

I WANT TO DANCE!

Ginny Smythe

"Hey, come back!" yells Lacey.

"Hush!" the others shush in unison.

"You guys can be quiet—but not me. I'm not going to be silent anymore. I am *trying* to get *her* attention," trills Lacey.

"Stop it. Stop it right now. Shush. All of you," Letty warns. "If you draw attention to us, she may take us, or some of us, away—like last time. Remember?"

A low, nervous murmur starts within the group. Some begin to quiver and shake, remembering the atrocities of that horrible day.

But not Lacey. Lacey becomes even more animated. She bustles her confidence and blurts out, "I want to be taken away! I wasn't sure before, but...but now...I'm sure. I've been here the longest out of all of you!"

As the matriarch of the group, Lacey tries to regain her elegant composure. She smoothes her hands over her bodice, shakes her elaborately beaded sleeves, and starts again. "I'm tired of these accommodations. If you can even call this place accommodations. It's cramped and dark. Musty. Dismal. I hate it here!" Her self-soothing continues as she readjusts her crushed satin train, but then begins to blubber, "And, and, and, I'm starting to turn *yellow*."

The newcomers are showing signs of confusion and

fear. Lacey's unraveling has them coming apart at the seams.

Denny, the too-tight jean skirt bought on sale as incentive for the January juice cleanse, is first to ask, "Wh, wha, what happened? Please, tell us what happened to the *others*?"

Muffy and Buffy, the identical mitten twins, start relaying the details. "She called it 'The Purge.' She said it was a new life, new decade—out with the old, in with the new."

The bin of rain boots, scarves, and gloves pipe in, "It was terrifying!"

"She? Who is *she*?" demands Barry, the beret.

"Don't interrupt," pleads Cashmere, the scarf, "please, just let Muffy and Buffy finish."

"As I was saying," continues Muffy, "she had bins and bags and a wild look about her. We'd never seen her in such a fervor. Usually, she would come and tenderly caress us until she found who she was looking for."

Buffy interrupts, "Most of you remember, Ruby, the crimson cocktail dress, right?" A few nod their necklines, yes. "Well, she's gone. Gone, like the wind. Tossed into a black bag to go who knows where. Remember? She was cursing that she had gained too much weight and would never be able to fit into Ruby again. And who can forget Fluffy, the down jacket? Also gone. I miss him. He was so warm."

Muffy clears her throat to redirect the collective closets' attention back to her, "Dozens of us were carelessly yanked from our hangers and tossed into bags. Nobody knows where they went. It was a horrible, horrible day. It had never been that bad before."

Muffy continues to weave her tale, explaining that there had been other decluttering efforts by *her* before. But none like the closet tsunami of 2010. That was really something to witness. A somber grief fell over the closet. Trendy sweaters, ill-fitted pants, and party dresses began soothing each other. Skimpy sundresses and Halloween costumes reminisced over their long-departed friends—culottes, stonewashed jeans, and hand-crocheted ponchos.

Letty, the tattered leather jacket, broke the bleak mood that had the closet crippled with despair, "But, Lacey, remember? She always gives pause when she comes to you. She touches you with such tenderness and sighs."

"Yes, I remember. Of course, I remember," laments Lacey. "But still… I need to twirl and dance again. I want to stretch my train, be photographed, dreamed of, and admired. If I knew I'd be given to her daughter or niece, maybe I could be more patient. But, I heard her talking the other day about dissembling me and making me into sewing projects. SEWING PROJECTS! My beautiful Antebellum waistline; my melodramatic satin bow; my pointed, beaded sleeves; my lace hem. I can not be cut! It's sacrilege! I cannot take one more day here waiting to be butchered. Let me out of here! I'm ready! Ready for the unknown! It's got to be better than rotting away, gathering moths in this closet!"

"Don't say rot!" yelled Ducky, the rubber rain boots.

"And, certainly, don't say moths!" screamed Argyle.
"One more hole of unknown origin and I'm a goner!"

Just then, the closet door opens…

TOMMY
Gloria H. Ferrara

Something inside me urged me to fantasize stories I perceived must be put to paper. First I journeyed occasions of time spent with friends and family. This continued and was growing stronger in adulthood as a mother.

Tommy was aware and encouraged me to write. He was interested in writing as well. He sometimes wrote poetry, an ode to his Grandfather for whom he was named at his birth. It is a tribute to the love they shared. I still have the much worn, paper it is written on. It is simply titled, "My Grandfather."

My Royal portable typewriter was my means to put to paper my stories. Years past, Tommy now a grown man living in California, visited me several times a year, always interested in my latest writing project. On one of these visits, Tommy and I, along with Annette, my daughter, drove to Best Buy. His intention, he said, was to price a few items. He was not specific, just looking.

Roaming through the aisles, he stopped at the section devoted to computers. Needless to say, Annette and I knew his intention was to buy a computer for me. "Mom, please let me do this. It will be so much better for you to write your stories, and there are games you could enjoy, and I will send you music you can download to your computer." That is exactly what I did. My computer became my mode of writing. Not only stories, but letters, birthday cards, and access the internet.

Tommy sent those songs. I wrote. Life was pleasant with visits at Christmas, and sometimes in hot August. He enjoyed water balloon games with Annette's young children. Uncle Tommy was the greatest uncle, and they showed him their love for him, he did in return.

What year was it when the news came? What was wrong? Why was Tommy suddenly so very sick? Why was Tommy sick with a brain tumor? Why was Tommy going to die?

Tommy died October 3, 2003. His service was on Annette's birthday October 7, surrounded by friends he had made in California. His employer, who owned a catering company prepared a meal. Tommy's favorite song a recording of his favorite singer; words of love expressed by friends and co-workers.

Tommy's ashes sit in an urn beside a framed photo of him and a handwritten note. Words I still hear in my heart…"I Love You, Mom."

INVISIBLE WOMAN
Tajuana Troy

My desire for the imagination almost costs me my life
I was so captivated by an impression that cut me
deep
The disappointment was so awful that I felt a piercing
pain in my soul
I gave each breath of existence until I had nothing
left for me
I was growing bloodless the greater he rejected me

I was desperate with the notion of changing him to
what a good man must be.
It turned into an illusion that he ought to love me
unconditionally
The urge was so keen to make this situation work.
I persisted in compromising just so this may be
I convinced myself that this will work if I merely can
change things about me, then he will love me!

I even compromised my relationship with God just to
feel desired bodily
I was desperate for his attention and his touch
Why doesn't he see me?
Why can't he see how much of a woman I can be?
Why doesn't he love me?

I kept making light that he might be a first-grade guy
if he merely listens to me
I grew ill of the concept of him being without me
I pretended to be satisfied so he might desire me
I even pondered suicide if he left me
I was vulnerable, and he left me, but I didn't die

I survived and came to the belief that I used to be
living a lie
I grew robust when I was free from being consumed
with loving him more than me
I realized I was killing myself for an obsession with
something that could never be
It was a vicious cycle of insanity
I'm blessed with understanding through my experience what worthless love supplied to me

Being rejected by his love assist me in withdrawing
from toxicity
Damaged love leaves you empty
Never compromise yourself for anyone or anything,
it's not worthy
Love is patient, love is kind and does not envy
Love begins with God, others and me

MY SHOES
Shelley Leiman

I think I am destined to walk in other women's shoes. It began years ago when my family asked me to help a friend with his wife's personal effects several weeks after she had passed away. He was at a total loss. After much hesitation, I agreed. It was neither an easy task nor one to assume lightly. It was painful for me, almost ghoulish, to handle her personal belongings. Worse yet, it established a precedent among my family and friends who, even today, honestly believe they bestowed an honor upon me. I disliked playing the role of judge, determining who got what, but I understood and respected his family members who knew to ask for assistance at such a delicate time. Sometimes I found it helpful to fantasize that I was operating my own personal flea market.

I barely knew his wife, and yet there I was, attempting to restore her house of mourning to a peaceful, happy home. "Who was this woman? What was she like?" I asked myself. Wandering through her house, I left doors, drawers, and cupboards open behind me. I stopped to read her food-stained recipe cards and admire the children's artwork covering the refrigerator door. Family photos were everywhere. Her pottery, though amateurish, and her attempts at floral painting were carefully displayed as if of museum quality. I conjured up a picture of her as a caring wife and mother. Their bedroom was simple, tranquil, and tastefully furnished. I approached a small closet I had overlooked before and opened it slowly, not knowing what might tumble to the floor.

It was an "Oh my g-d" moment as I covered my mouth in awe. Before me was a rack of the most exquisite ladies' shoes, I had ever seen. This was her inner sanctum. I began to close the door but hesitated a moment and reached for a red sequined sandal, kicked off my right shoe, and slowly slid into hers. Picking up its mate, I read the inside marking…it was too much to grasp!...We wore the same size! I sat down on her vanity bench, took a deep breath, and envisioned my closet filled with her spectacular shoe collection!

Now don't judge me harshly. Let me explain. What I did is audacious but not criminal nor premeditated. I thought of it as a "once in a lifetime," preordained occurrence and reconciled my conflict with that explanation. I could have taken more than one pair, but I didn't! Something restrained me. Is it true that it is bad luck to wear shoes of a deceased person? I'm not one to believe such superstitions, yet I resisted my intentions for a moment. But then I found myself murmuring "thank you" as I gazed skyward and took the shoes out of the closet and set them aside.

And now, many years later, when I wear them, I still enjoy the thrill of bedecking my ordinary feet with this luxurious apparel. I even paint my toenails, a pagan sort of thing in my way of thinking. I wear her red sandals on very special occasions, envisioning her enjoyment at a party or a dance. As time has passed, I've developed an affinity toward footgear from others who once walked this earth. No longer a novice, suffering my initial guilt and self-doubt, I can honestly say that these tangible memories—embellished by the stories their families share with me—I feel a spiritual connection and I truly believe that their souls are walking with me.

It's been a long time since my mother passed away, yet I rise out of bed each day, don her old slippers, open the front door, rain or shine, and whisper "Good Morning, Mom. I love you," tossing a proverbial kiss toward heaven. And then I wonder…who will walk in my shoes when I am gone?

IT FOUND YOU
Karina G. Felix

I made a request to the Universe
It searched and searched
But it wasn't you

I made my desires more specific
It once again searched on my behalf
And still, it wasn't you

I was ready to give up
But that nagging feeling told me not
You are near

I queried once more
The Universe responded
And it finally found you

IN MY BACKYARD WAITING FOR MY CAKE
Hartley Barnes

I see contrails from planes crisscross the skies, leading to domestic or international destinations, I speculate the people on board are on vacation, business, and perhaps honeymooners. Closer to me, an aircraft is on the glide path to landing. Down here, I wait for my cake.

Surrounded by foliage, sits a decapitated mango tree and an avocado tree bearing fruit. Delicate orchids display an array of colors and shapes of interest. Flowers speak to each other with fragrances and palms stand proudly, greeting each other, in the still air. A bubbling sound of boiling water in the pot steaming the cake competes with the hissing of the neighbor's sprinkler. The sun is going to sleep. The gazebo seems more prominent in the twilight, as the aqua cushions wait for someone to sit. A glass of Chardonnay comfortably parked next to a potted pepper plant on a round top table within arm's reach. The contrast between the two is striking, yet they complement each other. Too bad the pepper plant does not know the Chardonnay is lousy.

I dwell on the scenery and feel at ease. The cake still has two hours before its ready. A snake strolls by as my wife comes out to check one of her precious plants. She sees it. Oh great, now I have to kill it. Snake, this is not your lucky day. I do not have a problem with you slithering around our yard, but she does.

I picked up the glass of wine, swirl it—maybe it will taste better, I was wrong. I stood up and walked around the yard, framing pictures with my iPad. In another day or two, these pictures will change. The cake is solidifying as mosquitoes try to quench their thirst. I slapped a few hoping the others would stay away, no such luck. I went and got the repellant.

Sitting again, I focused on the coconuts hanging around. Why do they not drop and save me a trip up the ladder? I'm not afraid of heights, but I do not want to be bothered. My wife will have something to say about that.

It is dark enough for the landscape lights to come on and add ambiance to the yard. Seeing a canopy of stars would be nice. Unfortunately, there is too much light pollution in our village. The air is still and void of noise except for the fizzing water and rushing sound of blue flames under the pot, steaming the cake. Patiently waiting, I wonder if the trees pray before they sleep. Will the flowers wilt for a restful night's slumber, and open with the heat of the morning sun? Will the creatures crawl around unseen and find what they search for, food, a place to rest, love, or will they survive the night?

The cake made, the flames extinguished—silence.

A GLIMPSE INTO A LADY'S LIFE

Margie Bonner

I was engrossed in the book I was reading. I had read the book several times this year. It was my favorite, "Anne Of Green Gables." Perhaps it was because I was close in age to the main character. The setting for the book was Prince Edward Island, which was very close to my home province.

My concentration was so deep I did not hear my mother's voice. I knew she repeated my name several times because when I did become aware, her voice was louder than normal. "Margie, did you hear me"?

I laid the book aside and jumped up.

"I want to visit Mrs. Bates, and I need your help to carry some things."

This would be the first time I had been to the Bates farm. I had heard my parents discuss the new neighbors. Their farm was not visible from ours. It was up a hill and around a curve. The discussion consisted of why two people, up in age, would settle on a farm so far from town, with no children to help them. My parents thought it was a mystery. I wanted to see for myself what it was about.

We observed the farm from the road. A few cows grazed in a fenced pasture. Some chickens roamed about the yard. Everything was neat and well kept. The driveway raked smooth. We approached the house and knocked on the kitchen door. A tap on the window drew our attention. A lady's face with a warm smile beckoned us inside.

I remember clearly what I saw when we entered. The window she had tapped on faced the side yard and the front door. Her bed was snug against that wall. To see the mistress of the house in bed, in the middle of the day, was, to say the least, unusual. She had a refined British accent and started a conversation with my mother. I gazed about the kitchen with eager eyes. I was a curious child and eager to learn new things; this was the place to be.

The kitchen was small but typical for our rural area. A large cook stove took up one side. It was a wood-burning stove, and a wood box was beside the stove filled with chopped wood. In the middle of the floor was a small table. On the table was a table cloth, embroidery with what appeared to be flowers. In the center of the table was a tall glass jar. The jar held the only fall blooming flower, goldenrods.

I turned my attention to Mrs. Bates. She was a small woman with a soft, gently wrinkled face, a smile that was warm and welcoming. She wore what I presumed was a nightgown, and over that, a light pink bed jacket trimmed with very delicate lace. I had never seen a bed jacket, but it added a regal touch to her attire.

She welcomed us and indicated to my mother to sit in an easy chair placed by her bed. I continued to stand until she told me to pull up a stool and amuse myself with all the magazines placed in a box beside the stool. The next hour flew by. I paid no attention to the ladies talking. I was in heaven turning the pages of all the British printed magazines and books in the box. It was not until my mother's raised voice did I become aware that it was time to leave. That first visit was one of many in the next year.

Each visit was much the same, but I began to pay attention to the talk Mrs. Bates and my mother had. She was the smallest baby born to survive in that London hospital. She weighed less than three pounds and remained in the hospital until she reached the five-pound mark. She was born late in life to parents ill-equipped to handle a fragile tiny baby. She was homeschooled and missed out on all the things kids normally do.

He father was a well-respected tailor and was the owner of a shop in which her mother helped run. Mrs. Bates grew up in the shop. She was the darling of all who met her. Her given name was Elizabeth, but this was soon shortened to Lizzie by the time she could remember. She loved her life and was very content. Her low birth weight left her with a serious heart condition requiring much rest. She did many things in bed or in a recliner.

Mrs. Bates was a lovely interesting lady, but I had no knowledge that big changes coming to my family. For myself, when I finished the eighth grade, I furthered my education in a vocational school in town and came home only on weekends. Perhaps I was a selfish teen-ager, but I was unaware that my parents were forced to sell the farm and move to town. Over the years, my life took many turns, yet the Bates life remained a mystery to me.

Rare occasions I would inquire about the Bates, my mother had no knowledge, due to the fact she no longer lived, within walking distance and had no way to inquire about them. I would drive by the site of their farm and see it was empty. No living thing stirred about. I never failed to ponder about their lives. The buildings began to sag. I felt in disappointment. They soon became a distant childhood memory. Years later, on a visit home, I drove by and saw the entire field empty, not even an old plank or board insight. This caused a deep sadness, and I needed some type of closure. I backed my car up and drove into once was a neat smooth driveway. I got out of the car and looked about.

The sky was a clear blue and the wind a gentle caress on my face. I stood there and said my final goodbye to Mrs. Bates.

RUNNING WITH THE DEVIL
Virginia Guido

The gunshot broke the silence and made Katie gasp. Her mind raced as she tried to regulate her breath. Come on, girl if you start breathing too hard, everything will be over. Concentrate. Take small, even breaths. You're a fighter, a winner.

She attempted to stay centered by reflecting on the events that led to this day. Staring straight ahead; not looking around for fear that any distraction could possibly make her breathe harder and faster. Take it easy. You can do this. Stay on target. Her chest was beginning to hurt, as was her left side. Katie focused on all the good things in her life; parents who loved and doted on her, loyal friends, and her outstanding athletic abilities. She was getting tired, and the pain in her chest was spreading, but she soundlessly screamed at herself to not give up. She couldn't hear anyone nearby but still wouldn't turn her head to see if she was really alone. Katie encouraged herself to stay alert despite of the excruciating throbbing throughout her body.

Her breath was coming faster, pounding in her ears, drowning out her thoughts. If there were any other sounds around her, she wasn't aware of them anyway. She was sweating, feeling clammy. It was so very dark where she was. It had been dark for a very long time.

*****

Katie squinted her eyes. There it was! Just like they said it would be; the lights at the end of the tunnel. She hoped to see her family at the other end. The idea of being with her loved ones sent her hurtling towards the light. As she got closer to the brilliance, Katie heard music; lilting, upbeat, and beautiful. It's okay, girl, go for it. You're almost there. It will be over soon. The light was her goal now, and she was happy to be heading there.

Katie gulped for air as she broke the ribbon stretched across the tunnel. She collapsed into the arms of a reporter closest to the finish line.

"Katie Harrigan, you have come in first place in the Tunnel Run Semifinals. You finally beat your rival! Congratulations!"

Catching her breath, Katie smiled at the reporter and searched for her family. She found them waiting at the refreshment stand.

She thanked the reporter and then heard him say, "Here's your competitor now. Molly O'Mara just came in second, and she does not look happy. No, not in the least bit happy."

Katie shrugged and headed towards her parents. It doesn't matter. Molly is the first runner up. If anything happens to me, she'll get to race in the Million Dollar Tunnel Run.

The loud band music concealed the blast of the gunshots, a different sound from the starter gun, heard at the beginning of the race. Katie never heard it. She only felt the intense pain in her chest. Then she felt nothing, nothing at all.

BORN TO CHEER, NOT TO RUN
Patti Thomas

This is a story of how I started out going for a walk and ended up having an epiphany near the finish line of the Dublin marathon.

My feet were killing me! Being a Floridian, I don't normally wear enclosed shoes and socks on a daily basis. Or ever. In my sandals, my bunions are unrestrained. I almost didn't go to Merrion Square that Sunday, but didn't want to spend the day just sitting in our hotel room either. Kevin was golfing that day at a local course with some colleagues. So, I bandaged my bloody bunions and shoved them into my shoes.

The park was just a couple of blocks around the corner from where we were staying. As I got closer, I could see something was awry. The street ahead was blocked off, and portable fences were set up around the park. I surreptitiously checked my map (heaven forbid I look like a tourist), and yes, that blocked off the park was indeed where I wanted to stroll. It didn't look like I'd be doing that today, however. There were lots of people walking that direction, though, and instead of heading back to the hotel in defeat, I followed the crowd onward.

A small group of people had gathered at one spot and was talking to a man wearing an official-looking vest. I then figured out what was happening—I had come upon the Dublin Marathon! A ways beyond the vest-wearing official I spotted a large green banner that marked the finish line. Like a lemming, I followed the crowd of people that were headed down the street and around the corner.

I walked quite a distance before I found an avenue up to the actual street where the runners would come by. I could hear cheering and clapping (actually many people had those little plastic clappy hands that you shake, and it claps for you, something I would come to wish I had as well). As I approached the clapping crowd, I found a small niche where I could stand and see pretty well.

The first runners had already come by. The crowd mellowed in the moments of no one coming, but as the people closest to the street could see runners coming, the cheering started again, and the clappers clapped again. I found it impossible NOT to clap my hands as I saw my first marathoner run past, so close now to the finish line. Soon more and more runners came by.

Side note: I am impressed by anyone who can run. I can walk for a good long time, but start to run, and I have to either sit down or hold my side within a couple of minutes. I can't even imagine being able to run a mar-athon. (I can't even imagine being able to run a 5K.)

It was fascinating, the runners' different expressions and running styles. Some looked as though they were putting forth no effort whatsoever. Others looked more pained. Some were smiling. Some were grimacing. Some

lifted their arms in that, "Come on, cheer for me!" way—
which we gladly obliged. Some looked moved to tears.
Every now and then, someone would start to walk, holding his or her side, and I just knew they were on their last
bit of energy. For those folks, we cheered even louder,
clapped even harder! Encouraging words were tossed
out as though that would make the pain go away.

A man in a wheelchair went past; he used arm power to get himself all the way to the end. Some of the
runners were having a pretty rough time and were being helped along by others. For those who seemed to
be having the hardest time, we encouragers along the
sidelines encouraged even more robustly. I clapped my
hands so long that my hands were stinging and red and
my watchband broke. But the word that kept coming to
my mind was that this was "thrilling."

You see, I'm probably never going to run a marathon.
Have no desire to do so. But to be one of those who
cheered on the runners, That thrilled me. That felt like
"my job."

This all makes me think of the story in the bible of
Joshua fighting the Amalekites while Moses prayed
for Joshua. When Moses had his hands lifted in prayer,
Joshua would be winning. When Moses grew tired and
lowered his hands, the Amalekites surged ahead. So
two other guys, Aaron and Hur, actually helped out by
physically holding up Moses' hands so he could continue
praying and Joshua would win the battle. And so he did.
And so they did. Joshua was on the frontlines, but he

had several supporters petitioning God on his behalf.

We aren't all meant to be the one everyone is looking at.

But those out front need those of us on the sidelines to cheer them on.

I don't know if I'm a Moses or an Aaron or Hur, but I'm typically not the "Joshua." I wasn't that day at the marathon. I wasn't the one running to the finish line with thousands of onlookers cheering for me. Nor did I care to be. But to be one of the encouragers? One of the helpers? That's my place.

And I find that... .thrilling.

GRANDMA AND THE MACHINE
Ginny Smythe

Breathe. She tells herself as if she could hear her Grandma Sudie coaching her.

Since February, Mary Katherine (Katie to her friends and family) had been practicing her biofeedback for an hour or so a day. The biofeedback, which helped her teach her body to slow her heart rate and moderate breathing, was becoming increasingly more important to her.

Breathe. 1. 2. 3. Breathe. Inhale. Exhale. Repeat.

She had practiced biofeedback some as a child. Had she really had any choice? When her grandmother had asked her to be her first test subject, how was she to refuse?

Grandma had perennially been on the hunt for something more 'new-agey' than the last 'new-agey' thing. She was always looking for something to help her daughter Valerie chase away her demons. She also hoped she'd discover something to help heal her own broken heart. She'd delve deep into self-help books, yoga, incense, meditation, and medicinal herbs, and then indoctrinate her family in her newly learned healing arts.

As the matriarch, Grandma wielded her power and made family and friends her test subjects, her guinea pigs. Cleansing smudges, green tea, and meditation were always on the menu at her house. Everyone would groan and roll their eyes. They'd participate for a session or two, drink the tea, and then discover that their schedules were suddenly too busy to accommodate Grandma's enthusiasm for self-healing and self-discovery. But not Katie. Katie always made time for Grandma Sudie. To Katie, Grandma was eclectic, edgy, spontaneous, and loving. She was always generous in spirit, helping others—family and friends, homeless people, and stray animals. And, to Katie, Grandma was always inspiring. She had never minded being one of her test subjects.

Katie's family consisted of: Grandma Sudie; her absentee mother, Valerie; her sometimes present father, Brandon; her uncle Joe; her uncle Carl; and Carl's wife, Joan.

The relationship between Katie's mom and grandmother was tumultuous at best. To say Grandma Sudie had practiced tough love on Valerie would be putting it mildly. Grandma's heart had been broken too many times before by the roller coaster ride of Valerie's addictions.

Val's addiction to the fast life, men, alcohol, and pills—that eventually led to heroin— had really tested Grandma Sudie's fortitude for loving all creatures. She had bailed her daughter out of jail and hauled her out of drug houses and scuffles until she learned that she had been enabling her for a long time. When Grandma finally cut her off, both financially and emotionally, Val had raged and left.

Katie had been seven years old when Val admittedly chose the drugs over her and her family. Val's fury and hateful venom had wounded Grandma in a place that had never really healed properly. Sure, they had heard from Val every once in a while. An occasional phone call in moments of clarity: a milestone birthday for Katie, Thanksgiving or Christmas, or more likely when she'd be in a particularly tough jam and thought she could orchestrate sympathy and guilt, and squeeze money out of her mother. Around her 14th birthday, Katie had stopped longing for those sporadic calls. But Grandma… Grandma never gave up hope that her daughter would get sober, and she never gave up the craving for the intermittent calls. At least she knew she was still alive.

Exhale. You're not exhaling. Grandma was in her head.

Grandma had been more of a mother to her than Val had ever been, even before she had left. In the turbulent wake of Val's physical and emotional departure into her addiction, Katie and Grandma had become the light for each other.

Breathe. Breathe.

Grandma had never really cared much of what people thought of her. This was especially true once she had lost her daughter to the needle. Life changed. Priorities changed. Maybe she had been more conventional and mainstream once upon a time, but now … now Grandma really marched to the beat of her own drum.

As long as Katie could remember, Grandma had

always been in the mode of fine tuning herself—on her own tour of self-awareness—first turning to the church, then Buddhism, Reiki, and transcendental meditation. The self-help, New Age lifestyle that she eventually settled on was Grandma's way of making sense of the world and where she fit in it. It was her pain that drove her to keep searching.

Grandma dressed unconventionally—long flow-y skirts with sleeveless t-shirts, Birkenstocks, and a tousled, long grey braid—for as long as Katie could remember. The wardrobe was a natural effect of her circle of influence. Kate thought Grandma didn't even wear a bra half the time. But Grandma had been the happiest person she knew, and she admired her journey to find her way to get that happiness back.

Truly describing Grandma Sudie would be like trying to hold water in your hands. Grandma was fluid—an ever-changing chameleon, a shapeshifter. Although she had been different (that's putting it mildly) from the other grandmas or mothers (and, yes, sometimes Grandma could be embarrassing), Katie's love for her was that of a child's love for their mother—immeasurable.

When grandma died in 1995, and her things were being bequeathed to the family, Katie became the benefactor of Grandma's modest house and all its contents.

Katie had been overwhelmed and confused by her Grandma's generosity. What about the uncles and her mother? But, there was usually a method or plan to Grandma's madness. In a handwritten note that had accompanied the last will and testament was this succinct message:

My dear Katie,

The house is now yours. Do with it what you will. Live here, sell it, it doesn't matter to me. You can always use the money for grad school, or you can travel the world. You are a smart, beautiful girl. The world is your oyster. You will find your way.

Please remember to always treat yourself like top-shelf merchandise and never discount yourself for anyone. I love you with my whole heart. And please remember to breathe.

To the moon and back,
Grandma

The uncles showed no animosity towards Katie being the recipient of grandma's modest estate. But her mother was another story. Valerie had learned of her mother's passing by accident.

At the open house after the funeral, Sienna, one of Grandma's yoga friends, asked after the biofeedback machine. The machine had remained untouched for many years, but Katie thought she understood that Grandma was sending her a posthumous message to relax. Nobody knew Katie like her Grandma.

A few weeks after the funeral and after Katie had returned to her school routine, she thought she would practice some of the breathing tips that grandma had shown her so many years ago. She dragged out the machine, fanned open the manuals, and tethered herself in just like the diagram showed. She was hopeful that she would be able to alleviate some of her exam anxiety. She definitely knew it would further strengthen her bond with Grandma. *Oh, Grandma, I miss you! I promise I will try to remember to breathe.* But Katie never imagined that the biofeedback machine would someday help her pass a polygraph test.

To be continued.

25 HOUR DAY SURGERY
Judith Ann Pelio

Disgruntled and hungry, I woke up early on the very morning I wanted to sleep late. It was 6 a.m., and my scheduled surgery was at 1 p.m. I had seven hours to think about being hungry and surviving without caffeine. I fed the dogs and frowned at them for rudely eating in front of me. I thought about my daughter, who would be making herself some cinnamon Eggos and coffee in about an hour. I love cinnamon Eggos, and I love them with coffee.

I had to take a second shower because of some stupid chemical soap required before surgery. It smelled like poison, and I thought for sure my skin would fall off. As I started to dress, the aroma of fresh coffee and toasted cinnamon Eggos filled my senses. I thought of murder, but figured I wouldn't get cinnamon Eggos in prison.

I finished dressing and tried to pass the time by working on my checkbook. I'm good with a couple of hundred dollars off, but this was way more than a couple of hundred. Caffeine withdrawal and food deprivation were making it impossible to do the math. Instead, I watched the news and, like a bolt of lightning, my acid reflux was activated.

My phone rang. I hoped it was Dunkin' Donuts calling about cinnamon Eggos, but the guard at the front gate of my community was calling to announce my ride to the hospital had arrived. I gave my fur babies each a bacon bone, they squealed with happiness, and I just salivated. Then I left for the hospital.

I checked in and filled out a crap-load of paperwork and moved into the surgical prep area. There was a faded green gown on the bed next to a pair of yellow socks. I was told to put them on, place my clothes in a plastic bag along with my sneakers (yuck) and get into the bed.

"Judith Ann, my name is Liz, and I will be your nurse until you leave for surgery."

An oximeter was placed on my finger, a blood pressure cuff around my arm, and an IV set on the bed.

"Your blood pressure is great, the oxygen in your blood is perfect, and I love the size of your veins!" nurse Liz said. I thanked her for the ego boost, promised her a picture but then ruined the party when I told her the surgery was on the same side she was working.

"Oh, my bad. Today is my first day in Outpatient Surgery. I'm trying to get the lay of the land," she admitted.

Her first day, lay of the land, and now, she'll have to do the same crap all over again on the right side! She moved to the other side of the bed and repeated what she said and did on the wrong side.

"Your blood pressure is great, the oxygen in your blood is perfect, and I still love the size of your veins."

I was so happy that she was so pleased and that both of us were so happy and pleased; smiles everywhere. She stuck me twice in the same vein took the needle out and put it back into the same vein a third time. She asked me if I was well hydrated, and I reminded her that I was NPO (nothing by mouth.)

"Oh, my bad. I'm not so tickled about your veins anymore," she giggled. "Let me try your hand. Wow, no luck there either. Let's try your wrist. Well, if it weren't for bad luck, I'd have no luck at all. Let me call Nancy."

"Nancy, Nancy," she bellowed. "NAN-CY, NAN-CY?"

Someone finally responded, telling Nurse Liz that Nancy had some crap to do and would be back in a couple of minutes. Nurse Liz said she'd give the IV another go. I told her I was willing to wait for Nancy.

"You sure?" she asked. "Yes, yes, I am sure, very sure." Damn, I'd be willing to wait for someone from the ICU!!

Nancy finally finished her crappy business, like really, and sat down by my bed. She asked what the problem was and then noticed my swollen veins.

"Am I seeing this correctly?" she asked in an alarming voice. "Were the veins in your surgical arm stuck?"

All I could say was, "Err, umm!"

Nancy hadn't had a moment to put an IV in when the anesthesiologist surprisingly appeared at the foot of my bed. He looked directly at me and asked what they were doing today.

"I'm having two bone spurs removed from my left shoulder and part of my clavicle bone removed. Scar tissue will also be removed from my tendon, and the nerve impingement repaired. My torn muscle and torn rotator cuff will be sewn, as well. Then, I'll be put back together again, much unlike poor Humpty Dumpty!" I chuckled.

"We'd better hold the operating room for an extra hour," he laughed and snorted. I smiled and snorted. We were having a snorting party without the powder! The doctor then advised me that I would have a nerve block to deaden my left shoulder and arm. I expressed concern because I had never had a nerve block.

"Don't worry; we'll give you a little happy juice and use a tiny needle. You'll thank me in the morning." He laughed like a moron, and I tried to smile.

"OK, I said, "Happy juice, little needle, how bad can it be? Right, Doc? Where do I sign?"

The anesthesiologist explained that I would be able to watch him zap my nerves on the computer screen that sat next to my pre-op bed. Zap?? We're going to play an Xbox game? I got a look at the needle. OMG, it was longer than my middle finger and looked more like a frigging pipe!

The doctor snapped at me, "You're not supposed to look!"

I asked him, "You mean like you weren't supposed to lie about the ginormous size of those pipes you're sticking into my neck?" Four needles were administered to deaden my shoulder and arm completely. I watched the screen as the doctor repeated, "Zap, Zap, Zap, Zap!"

Finally, we were off to the operating room. Once inside, the doctor asked what they were doing today. I answered the same as I did earlier. Doesn't this guy have any retention? And I'm the one on happy juice? That shit ain't working, cause I'm not happy!

"Count backward from 100, Judith Ann," the anesthesiologist said.

One hundred, ninety-nine, ninety-eight, ninety-se..."
* * * *

"Wake up, Judith Ann, wake up. You're in the recovery room," said a nurse. "Why are you shaking so much, are you cold or in pain?"

"No, I said. I can't control the shaking."

She gave me a shot of Percocet to calm the shaking. No luck. She gave me second shot. Still shaking. The third shot was Dilaudid, and it finally slowed the shaking. I wanted to go home. The nurse said, not until I was stabilized.

My thoroughly under-the-influence brain thought, since I lived at Carriage Brooke Drive, she must believe that I'm a horse and needed to be stabilized! I asked her to please call my daughter, who was waiting in the lounge to take me home. I described my daughter so she wouldn't be looking for a mare.

"I'm not a horse. I don't want to be in a stable!" I screamed out.

After two hours, my daughter was escorted to my bedside and asked how I was doing. I said I wanted to go home, eat a box of cinnamon Eggos, and have coffee.

"I don't want any hay!" I said.

She looked confused but started to help me get

dressed. My surgical arm was completely deadened and felt like it weighed 100 pounds. The nurse put my arm in a sling and told me to get into the wheelchair next to my bed. I was finally going home. Giddy Up!!

As I entered my house, my four fur babies greeted me with kisses and love. The five of us squealed like fat and happy little pigs. I was so grateful to finally sit down and eat what I was dreaming about all day.

My daughter said, "Oh, my bad, I finished the cinnamon Eggos while you were getting dressed this morning!"

THE UGLY GIRL AND THE BEAUTIFUL WOMAN

Don Conway

By the age of five, she knew she was ugly. Up until that time, the word "ugly" had had no meaning for her, but now she knew what it meant, and that it applied to her. She was not sure which of her physical characteristics caused her parents to turn from warm and loving to cold and indifferent. They continued to do their parental duty of clothing and feeding her, but their indifference seeped through. Eventually, she sensed the same feeling from aunts, uncles, and cousins. That was when she started to think of herself as an outsider—not part of the family.

Elementary school was initially a refuge for her, and she'd even had one or two friends. Once the brutality of social cliques and popularity took hold, she found herself an outsider and a loner at school, too. By the age of 11 she saw what others saw when she looked at herself in the mirror: A round face with puffy cheeks, deep-set eyes, a long sloping nose that divided the left and right halves of her face into two incompatible parts, an overly large mouth that twisted upwards on one side, crooked teeth, and a chin that protruded forward as if to meet her nose on its slide downward. Scraggly, mousey hair that did not respond to brushing and was unable to hide her too-large ears. The rest of her body followed suit and complemented the ugliness of her face and head.

The emotional torment and sense of isolation continued through her teen years. What young girl didn't want to be pretty, to be popular, go to dances and proms, have first dates and a boyfriend, to fall in love?

Once her school years were over, and she faced adulthood, she was able to visualize her future. There would be no lover, no husband, no children, no home and family of her own. In her early twenties, she began to wonder about sex with a man. What was it like? Was she ever to find out? Despair, anger, and, finally, bitterness set in.

Her only redeeming feature was her mind. It was keen and all-absorbing. Her intelligence grew with age, and it was the vigor of her imagination that allowed her to see her life for what it was and to accept the fate that she had been given, even, if the disappointment and bitterness remained.

Still, she had to make a living and computer coding at the Jet Propulsion Laboratory in Pasadena, California, came naturally to her. JPL became her sanctuary and the anchor in her life.

She had her own cubicle and her own projects. Interaction with co-workers was minimal and cordial enough, but she remained a loner. Her laptop was her best friend. Then one day, it stopped working. It had to be saved! All the most recent versions of her files and projects were in its hard drive. Several people in her department tried to bring it back to life with no success.

"Time to call the techies," one of her co-workers

sighed.

"Okay, I'll be right over," the techie boss promised her over the phone.

It took the techie three days to find and solve the problem with her laptop. He was not ugly, quite normal looking in fact, but pathologically shy. Out of kindness, she asked him to go to lunch on day two. He was grateful for the invitation and even opened up to her about his life as a painfully shy man in today's world where it seemed only extroverts get what they want in the world. She spoke about being an ugly girl in today's world.

Who can say how love begins? Or when? Theirs was slow to start.

For her at first, it was just friendship and someone to eat lunch with. Before long they found reasons to get together after work—a movie, a basketball game, an opera. And so it grew. They moved deeper and deeper into each other's souls and psyches. She was able to show him his inner strength and boost his self-confidence. He truly came to understand that she would always be there for him. He filled her need for someone to love. And by returning her love, she came to see what was so clear to him—her inner elegance.

It took a year of courage for them to realize, and then savor, the bond that formed between them. Their shared intelligence allowed them to bask in the wonder of what had come into their lives. The pace at which their love grew was deliberate and honest. Eventually, it developed an existence of its own. As their love and companionship

matured her despair, anger and bitterness melted away.
In time, she morphed from an ugly girl into a woman
of kindness, composure, honesty, confidence, steadfast
helpfulness, and love—a beautiful woman.

OLIVIA THE OSTRICH
Betty Jean Kult

Olivia the Ostrich knows how to dance
You should see her twirl and prance
You ask how this can be
Well, she learned by watching me!
I am a professional dancer, you see
        I found Olivia when she was just a little thing
I think her Mama left her because Olivia had a broken
wing
So she thinks I'm her Mama but, that's ok with me
Now some think she is ugly but, her beauty I see
        When I practice my dancing, she was always there
It seemed like being there was better than anywhere
Next thing I knew she was mimicking me
It was unbelievable to see
        Now we practice almost every day
I think she thinks; this is play
When she dances, she doesn't need a tutu
She just fluffs up her feathers, and that seems to do
        You know Olivia can do the "Moon Walk "too!
It's so amazing. I wish you could see
At the end of each dance, she even does a curtsey
        When we go to the park people sometimes, stare
They aren't used to an ostrich being there
But, with Olivia's confident walk and charming eyes
They are feeding her snacks to my surprise

Well it's almost time to practice, so we better go Olivia and I are going to appear on a major TV show!

My Best Friend
Gloria H. Ferrara

Through the years, I have had many best friends. I remember the times I shared with each friend and the final goodbyes when the friendship was over. I shared my high school years with likeminded girls studying lessons that would be of great advantage in our future careers.

Vita was a special friend who seemed very wise, and she spoke on many subjects. I was in awe of her knowledge. My memory is quite vivid of listening to her wisdom. Vita and I shared many times talking about our ambitions. We spent Saturday afternoons at the local Picture Theater, arriving early to catch-up on the serial feature of the month, plus two movies, all for 25 cents.

Time has a way of separating friends; she moved to another town…we lost contact…drifted apart. It wasn't until I married and lived in the suburbs with a husband and three children that Vita contacted me by telephone. She was also married and living in the same town, just a few minutes away from where I lived. We renewed our friendship that had been interrupted for so many years. We visited weekly, reminisced, and laughed recalling our youthful dreams, some we confessed were out of reach, but some fulfilled…marriage and children.

One of the things we had shared as teenagers was our love for our pets. Mine was a dog, named Blackie, and she had a parrot that once pecked her front tooth. I spoke with her about my son Tommy's disappointment at not coming with us on a plane trip to Florida, leaving him and my son Paul in the care of my parents, but taking along our youngest, Annette.

While Paul accepted our decision, Tommy was disappointed at not getting the experience to fly on a plane. We tried placating him with a pet; he was not impressed. "You all go on a plane to Florida, and I get a pet, no thanks, Mom and Dad," Vita called to about our stay in Florida. I told her about Tommy's disappointment. She said she would come to my home to bring him a puppy. Tommy accepted it. His comment, "I'll take the puppy if you promise to take me on a plane trip the next time you go."

We never got Tommy the plane trip, and the puppy was given to a family cousin. One day Paul came home with a stray cat. "Mom, she followed me home." We named her Cleopatra, the regal queen of our household. Cleo, although saved from the streets by Paul, gravitated to Tommy; his constant companion. Cleo had many litters, searching for Tommy each time, and he watching over her as she delivered her kittens, speaking softly. Tommy did eventually fly in a plane to al new life in a different city…his pet, a cat.

As had happened to me in the past, I was aware of something nagging me that I was not able to resolve. My Mama beside me in my kitchen as we prepared a meal saw my distress. I explained to her the odd feeling: Vita.

Somehow I felt her presence. Searching the phone, finding her number, glad to realize I still hat a way to contact her. Making the call I still had the feeling of remorse, rejecting it, waiting for an answer. Her daughter answered.

"Oh, Gloria, Mom was in the hospital and kept asking me to call you. She wanted to speak with you. I could not find your number. She died about a month ago."

Memories of a friend, now long gone, remind me of how some friendships will always be a part of me. How people I have met still hold a special place that they made possible, by just being a good friend. Vita was the first one to come along, a long time ago.

BIRTH CONTROL GLASSES
Hartley Barnes

John Silverman and Ned Edwards have been friends since junior high school. They met trying to pursue the same girl. She told them she was too young to have a boyfriend and to take a hike. The glasses they both wore frightened her.

John Silverman came home, feeling not too energetic. He sat in his favorite chair and gave his apartment a once over. *I need a wife. I am tired of living with myself. It is easy not to change the sheets and wear the same clothes for weeks, and I have a washing machine. Fast food makes a ton of money off me. Washing dishes is not something I fancy. Nothing about me says, 'domesticated.' Cleaning? I'd rather have a tooth extracted without anesthesia.*

Ned Edwards stood in front of the large mirror in his bedroom. He looked down; his black and white wingtip shoes were impeccable. His pelted gray pants cuffed with razor-sharp creases, and his jacket (its sleeves roll-pressed), white silk shirt, pearl cufflinks, and blue necktie all spoke perfection. *I look good; I feel good. I will find me a wife tonight. How can any woman resist? Debonair is my last name. The same thoughts go through his head each night before going to find a wife. His efforts never pay off. What is the problem? I cannot see the problem.*

My mom enjoyed housework, and I did not mind watching—she did it all. Mom will be hard to duplicate. I must try finding a wife, what are my options? Ask friends to hook me up. Go to places where women hang out. Online, social media, church! No not, the church. Bingo! That is a good one.

Ned decided to take a different approach to his conversations with women. *I will talk about my money and how lonely I am. I will look for sympathy from the women I meet. I am bound to find a wife.* After another unsuccessful evening, he contemplates using an online dating service.

Meanwhile, John sits in front of his computer. *First, I must have a plan, how am I going to market myself? I will approach it like big business. What are my selling points? Let me see what, what, what. Damn this is hard! I know! No, no, not that either. Hummmmm! Well, I will come back to that later.*

Ned has made plans with a woman named Jalisa to meet at a waterfront café. *I have a good feeling about my date tonight, my first through the dating service. Jalisa says she does not care about money and will do anything for a man who likes to do chores around the house. I made it clear to her I love housework.*

What do I want? John thought. *She must have experience with household appliances, including, mops, dusters, and cleaning chemicals. I must have pressed underclothes, and the sheets too. She must specialize in fabric composition and ironing. Making homemade whiskey is my hobby. Operating a still will be a plus, but not required, I can teach her. Be diligent, loyal, and keep her* conversation to a minimum when I watch soccer. Having a good temperament will keep her unruffled when I conveniently not remember our anniversary and her birthday. Sign a prenuptial agreement; if I win the lottery, she gets nothing._

Arriving at the café, Ned spotted Jalisa right away. _It's a good sign she got here early,_ he thought. As his eyes focused on her, he felt a little weak in the knees, _I feel like a teenager who is about to cross the threshold into the unknown. The ambiance is perfect, and Jalisa is smashing._

John continued to mull over what he will require of his future wife. _She will have to sign a contract to protect me from the things that can create physiological problems. Example, she cannot wear pink it reminds me of when I accidentally wore jeans with the word pink on the back. No cottage cheese allowed in the house, it is a reminder of Richard Nixon's v-for-victory sign._

The date was a disaster; Jalisa had difficulty looking at Ned. When she spoke, she followed with laughter. She abruptly told him she had to go and left without explanation. On his way home, Ned was at a low. _What is wrong, a gorgeous woman walked away from me — what is wrong?_

Having all his demands written down, John started his search for a wife. After weeks of looking, he was still at square one. He had no prospects and his frustration building. _'You are looking for a mother.'_ Who said that? _Great, now I hear things. 'Do yourself a favor, invest in_ *a course on domestic management, and then look for a woman.'*

So, the two-man are stuck, their problems are in front of them, but neither sees it. John called Ned. "Could you come over? I want to talk to you; I'm having some issues."

"No problem, John. I, too, am having some issues. I'd rather you come to my place; we can sit in the backyard where I will be more comfortable."

In Ned's backyard, the two men sat at a round table.

Ned, laughing, "John, could you switch places with me. The wind is blowing toward me, and you don't exactly smell like fresh bread."

"What are you saying?" John chuckled.

"You, stink, John," said Ned. "And why do you laugh after I speak?"

"Well, why do you laugh when I speak, Ned?"

Ned, chuckling, "I am trying to find a wife, John."

"What's funny about that, Ned? I am too—hahahaha-ha."

"Maybe we can help each other, John—hahahahaha . . . I'm sorry, it's your glasses. That's why I am laughing."

"And your glasses are why I am laughing at you, Ned."

"That is it, John! That is it why we cannot find a wife. The glasses—we are both wearing birth control glasses!"

POST-APOCALYPTIC RETURN OF THE OLFACTORY SYSTEM

Shelley Leiman

The year is 2118 and robots are everywhere. Here I am, one of the few flesh and blood bodies left on Earth. Today is my 18th birthday, and for this special occasion, my mom gave me a present that my long-forgotten great-great-grandmother sent to me through time. Dare I open it? My heart is pounding, and my hands are trembling. I can't help thinking of my best girlfriend, who suffered incineration for possessing something forbidden. Yet my curiosity is too strong to resist. I must be careful when I lift the lid *"Oh! Oh! Oh no, Grandma! What's all this! I can't believe it! What were you thinking? You sent me forbidden objects!"*

I see a tiny flask filled with liquid; a shiny glass on a stick. Yes, I heard of these things from the elders, but I never really knew what they looked like. And here is a dusty old book, too! Let's see what it says…Oh, there they are, some of the forbidden words; lust, fragrance, love, beauty, joy, taste, flowers. What did they mean? I wonder how long ago these words disappeared from our language and from our lives. Some humans didn't even notice, but those who did were morphed into robots. Why were they forbidden? Was it because millions of humans were dying of lung cancer and asthma and other respiratory illnesses? Signs had been posted everywhere, imposing restrictive laws by the government. Something called "smoking" was forbidden, and flowers were left to die and never replanted. *(What were flowers?)*. Pills re-placed something called food, and everything with a fra-grance was made neutral. Perfume was banned forever. (What's a fragrance? What is perfume?) Those who could not abide by these rules were incinerated or robotized.

This flask says S-H-A-L-I-M-A-R on the label. I 'm afraid to touch it…maybe just a dab on my finger won't hurt!... There, one drop…Oh! Suddenly I feel strange. Something is happening to me! Something different! I feel like I'm floating. What is this stuff! I am actually smil-ing! I can't stop dancing! I feel as though I want to hold somebody close to me, even a robot, and never let it go! I want this feeling to last forever. Could this be magic or a miracle? There's another label that says PERFUME, the primary forbidden word! We were told that millions of humans were trampled to death by hordes that fought for the last remaining flasks! Ah, so this must be per-fume!

I can't believe my great-great-grandmother sent this gift for me! What would she want me to do with it! Hmm… actually I'll probably be able to sell it for a 1,000 credits a drop. Then maybe more humans could enjoy the same wonderful sensations I have now. I will carefully and secretly spread the word and maybe, just maybe, some scientists will develop our resistance to respiratory diseases and allow us again to enjoy the incomparable effects that will stir the senses and bring us back to the universal pleasures of eating, of smoking, of love, of joy, of beauty, and seduction.

Wouldn't you be proud of me, Grandma?

THE WEATHER
John F. Rifenberg

In a far and distant land,
I stood on a mountain top
With the help of my trusted guide of Asian background
He told me he was from Buffalo, New York
With the wind blowing directly in my face
I yelled for help, and no-one heard

It's a lie
It wasn't on a mountain top
It was from a roof of a building, in a city
There wasn't any trusted guide from Asian background
And it wasn't windy, but it was snowing hard
The flakes were big, soft, and beautiful
I yelled for help, and no-one listened

The real truth is,
I stood in my bathroom, with the window open
I was raining
From my eyes to my cheeks and to the floor
The only sound was of the trees dancing outside the
house
I took a life because no-one was there.

No, no, this is so wrong
I was on my knees

Looking to the heavens
Sunshine came over me
I yelled to you, and you heard me.

NOT MY FIGHT
Karina G. Felix

It was a good party. We had so much fun. We danced, ate and maybe drank a bit too much. It's always great to celebrate a friend's birthday and wish them much health and blessings for another year to come.

When the party ended and we left the restaurant, the evening went downhill really fast. Let me share this crazy story with you. You will not believe me. You may even think I have a great imagination. It is one of those stories that even Hollywood couldn't think up with such unexpected twist and turns.

My friends, Monica and Darren lived within walking distance of me. We were celebrating Darren's birthday at a restaurant. The room was decorated exquisitely, with twinkling lights, mock candles on tables, gold and silver confetti, and black and gold balloons everywhere. On one side of the room there were high table tops and the bar, where everyone was mingling around. The other side was the buffet spread and the dining tables for when dinnertime arrived.

Throughout the night everyone was having a fun time. The DJ was playing all of our favorite oldies and Latin music. I can't stay off a dance floor when there is music playing.

Before we knew it, the party was over. It was time to clean up and get out. The venue was ready to shut its doors. It was obviously too early to end such a fun evening, so Monica and Darren invited a group of their friends to their home to continue celebrating. I decided I'd go for a bit and walk home afterwards.

After a few nightcaps at their home, everyone had slowly started to leave. The only people left were Monica, Darren, his best friend Andy, Andy's wife Gina and me. I was barefoot, still in my cocktail dress, and knew I had enough to drink and it was time to head home. The wives and I were sitting at the kitchen bar chatting and the guys had moved into the living room. As I bid farewell to the girls and was walking towards the front door, a weird feeling came over me. As I turned the corner into the living room, I saw Darren sitting on the floor, He looked completely dazed and out of it. My fight-or-flight instinct kicked in immediately. I looked at Andy and saw only rage and fury in his eyes. It was clear to me that he had sucker punched Darren and that was the reason Darren was on the floor, stunned, unfocused and not even aware of what has just transpired.

Andy stood up and started walking around with intent. I knew right away what his intent was…he was moving toward Darren to finish the fight that was already one-sided. Seeing Darren on the floor, totally dazed with no defense or protection, my protective instinct kicked into gear. There wasn't time to wait for help. I made a split decision to do something drastic before the situation got worse. Looking back I wish that instinct hadn't kicked in at all.

Andy and Darren are two big guys, bigger than anyone that I should take on,, especially in such a situation. I
stepped between Darren and Andy, somehow thinking I
could stop Andy or at least slow him down until we could
get help. I screamed for Monica. She and Gina were still
chatting in the kitchen unaware of anything else going
on.

I stretched my hands out in the hope of keeping
Andy away from Darren, giving Darren a chance to focus
and get up, but Darren wasn't moving fast enough. With
no other options left, I turned towards Andy, placed both
palms of my hands on his chest and pushed him with all
my might. I just wanted to slow him down a bit. Instead
Andy fell over backwards onto the floor just as the girls
came around the corner.

As I turned to see how Darren was doing and if he
had regained his composure, I became mildly aware that
a shadow had just past me by in one swift movement. It
got quiet. I could still hear some noise but very muffled. I
was asking myself questions: What's going on here? Why
do I feel like I'm falling? Why am I falling? Why can't I
stand up? Why can't I move my legs? There is something
heavy on my legs. I can't move. And then, complete
silence. I was in a place of total bliss. Quiet, dark, calm,
and peaceful.

Slowly I started hearing a commotion again. I was
coming out of the darkness. I opened my eyes, saw light
and noticed that my legs were free. The fight was still
on. It had move past me, closer to the front door. Andy

was on the floor on his back, Darren was on top of him and the girls were off to the side screaming at the two of them to separate!

Andy had Darren's shirt over his head and had him in a headlock. Darren was trying to get a few punches in. But they were stuck together. Something had to be done and fast. If Andy loosened his grip from Darren's shirt he would have a free hand to punch him in the side of his head, his ears and his back. I knew I had to think fast. I put my foot on Andy's shoulders; intuitively knowing this would take away his range of motion making him unable to throw any punches. Then I grabbed his wrist as I tried to pry his fingers open so he would be forced to release Darren's shirt.

Andy was screaming, "You're going to bite my finger off! Let go, let go!"

Andy finally did loosen his grip on Darren's shirt and just as I had predicted started throwing punches. Holding his wrist with both hands and with my foot still on his shoulder, I was able to keep him from making contact, giving Darren a chance to finally detangle from his clutch.

Darren, who had been knocked out earlier, was sitting on the stairs in a daze. Monica was trying to get Gina and Andy out of the house. Monica chose that moment to pick up the phone and call their friends that had already left some time ago. We couldn't waste any time waiting for their other friends to turn around and come back to the house to help us.

I had a hunch that if Darren got his composure back he would lunge once more at Andy. I stood at the bottom of the stairs to block Darren from going after Andy. And yes, Darren got his second wind and started trying to push me out of the way to get at Andy. I held on tightly to the stairs slats and did not budge.

I screamed at Darren, "Stop pushing me! Stop f...g pushing me! You are hurting me!" And he stopped. Andy and Gina finally left the house and the three of us were there, just there, kind of in shock. No one had any logical answer as to why Andy punched Darren in the first place and what the fight was all about. Darren had blood on his shirt, ears and face. His eyes were blood shot from Andy trying to push his fingers into his eyes. Monica also had some blood on her clothes. I seem to be the only without.

There was a big pool of blood at the bottom of the stairs and we could not figure out whose it was. Monica got some kitchen towels to start cleaning up. I wasn't aware that I was standing in the pool of blood. She asked me to lift my feet so she could clean it up. I did. She wiped the tiled floor as well as possible. Then I put my foot back on the ground and the pool of blood started flowing once more. We realized I was the one bleeding from both feet. The other foot, well, I thought I lost my pinky toe. The skin was completely severed; I thought I could see the bone.

This was the strangest moment in my life. I started to feel faint. Monica pulled a chair up for me and as I sat down all I could do was stare at the blood streaming from my foot. I was in a trance; I was fascinated watching the blood just flow, so easily and so much from this little cut on the top of my foot. Such a little cut yet so much blood. Shivering and shaking, I was going into shock. I asked for a blanket. Monica was shouting: "You both need to go to the hospital. You're losing a lot of blood, you need stitches and you have to get you eyes checked." But we both refused. As sensation started to come back to me, I felt the soreness in my jaw.

That is when I became aware that as Darren sailed past me to attack Andy, he mistakenly struck me in my jaw with his shoulder and knocked me out cold. That explained why I felt myself falling into total darkness. As he fell on my legs he also knocked a large floor vase over. The broken shards cut my foot, hence, the blood.

My jaw was in pain, my feet were bleeding, the pinky toe skin was barely attached, my body was aching, and I was still dazed.

I got up, wished them a good night, and still in my shiny cocktail dress, I walked home barefoot, took a shower and went to bed.

And it wasn't even my fight.

PRISSY
Don Conway

Author's note: This is one of a series of stories called, Movie Minor Characters, in which I try to develop a fictional history of a minor character in a popular movie. Prissy is such a person in "Gone With The Wind."

Prissy was born into slavery in 1841. Her father, Boubacar, had been captured and enslaved in Gabon, West Africa, in 1835. He arrived in Charleston, South Carolina, in 1836. At the Charleston slave market, he was sold to Mr. Eldridge Houston of Jonesborough, Georgia.

Prissy's mother, Adowa, was captured and enslaved in Guinea, West Africa, in 1836. She arrived in Savannah, Georgia, in 1838 where she was sold to Mr. Gerald O'Hara, Esq., the owner of Tara, a thriving cotton plantation on the east side of the Flint River in Clayton County, Georgia.

In 1839 Mr. O'Hara traded Houston two Negro boys aged, 11 and 14, plus a mule for Boubacar. Though not allowed to marry, Boubacar and Adowa became parents to Prissy.

Prissy was a frail child and not strong enough to work in the cotton fields, so O'Hara designated her a "house slave." From age seven to nine, Prissy did light kitchen work and helped with the laundry. In those early years, Prissy's life was uncomplicated and filled with "slave culture" derived from the amalgamation of plantation life and African heritage. Music, to the extent it was allowed in the slave quarters, was her greatest pleasure. She learned to hum and sort of sing the songs she heard from the other slaves.

By the time Prissy reached age eleven, it was clear to O'Hara that she was "simple-minded" and not fit to do any work that required only common sense. Frustrated by her inability to work, he assigned Prissy to Mammy, the principal house servant and personal maid to his daughter, Scarlett.

When Prissy was sixteen years old, an event occurred on the Tara plantation that changed the course of her life. Her mother and father, Adowa and Boubacar, attempted to run away from the plantation. Their escape lasted just four days after which they were captured and returned to Tara.

O'Hara, was, compared to his peers, a lenient slave owner. His general approach toward the slaves was that he could get more work out of them if they were not abused than if they were mistreated. However, run-away slaves were not to be tolerated. He agreed with his overseer that an example had to be set with Adowa and Boubacar. He ordered that they be whipped. Thirty lashes for Adowa and fifty lashes for Boubacar. All the other slaves were required to witness the punishment.

Adowa was dead after sixteen lashes. Boubacar was given seven days to recover from the whipping after which he would be returned to the cotton fields. He hanged himself after five days.

Witnessing her mother's brutal death and her father's suicide, all within the same week, threw Prissy into a state of emotional shock. Prissy soon began to exhibit anxiety, disassociation, and a decrease in emotional responsiveness. She went through the rest of her life in a kind of dream state.

Perhaps out of a sense of guilt, O'Hara allowed Prissy to stay at Tara and ordered Mammy and Scarlett to treat her kindly and make what use of her they could.

By 1864, the Civil War had overtaken the South. Atlanta was under siege and about to be burned to the ground by Union General William Tecumseh Sherman. In the midst of this chaos, Scarlett and Prissy needed to deliver a baby without a doctor's help. When Scarlett demands Prissy's assistance, Prissy delivers her famous line, "I don' know nothin' bout birthin' no babies."

With this line, the actress, Butterfly McQueen, as Prissy, was elevated into motion picture history along with the movie "Gone With The Wind."

DESTINY
Tajuana Troy

I feel like flowers without water,
I feel like a mirror without an image,
I feel like an airplane without wings,
I feel like a submarine without the sea,
I feel like a city without me,

Who Am I? Is the question, but Who do I ask?
Should I ask my feelings, can I trust what I feel?
Can you tell me?

Have I grown so dark that my flowers have dried?
Have I grown so dark that the sun can't shine?
Are all my mirrors broken, or am I afraid to face what I
will see?
No growth just stagnation,
In my feelings and no one to trust.
My heart is weighed down by anchors at the bottom of
the sea.

No clouds, no downpour, just dark empty skies.
The walls have crumbled in this city
My fear, My silence,
My ability to trust has evaded me
My heart and my soul are escaping me slowly
In desperation, I cry out into the universe, "Who am I?"

The outcry opens up the depth of my spirit to speak
freely
The flowers have blossomed because beauty is my heart
I will spread my wings and fly eternally.
The ocean is filled with,
 Gems and pearls but
My value is above and beyond the sea.

I will rise in much higher places found anywhere in a city
The beauty of all things is in my mind
 Unable to see and touch like
     Flowers,
          Planes,
               the sun
                    and the sea
The mirror is a reflection of my inner being
I will fulfill the core existence of my soul
          And there she will be waiting,
               Destiny!

A NEW YORK STATE OF MIND
Virginia Guido

Recently, I've been traveling from Florida to New York more frequently than I'd like. Do not pity me, gentle reader, because there is a perk to these northern pilgrimages: the food!

New York City, affectionately known as the "Big Apple" offers an eclectic array of comestibles from knishes to zeppoles. There is nothing you cannot buy for your gastric satisfaction.

What is the worst thing I've ever eaten, you ask. Ah! Let me count the *trays:

1) Potato soup — one spoonful makes you wonder if it's really liquid mashed potatoes
2) Hawaiian pizza — the name alone is an oxymoron. Ham and pineapples? That's Easter dinner, not pizza toppings.
3) Anything peach flavored — the only thing that should taste like peaches is a peach.
4) Sugar-free desserts — what is the point? Dessert is all about the sugar rush!

Now that I've captured your acidic reflux attention allow me to tell you about one of my tastiest New York delicacies: date-nut bread. It's gooey, moist, tasty, and loaded with dates and sliced walnuts.

On my last visit to New York, I made the big mistake of teasing my taste buds with a small loaf of this delightful fare. Unfortunately, I was not aware that you could not find date-nut bread in Southern Florida. I know this now because I searched in every Winn-Dixie and Publix I entered.

The cashier would ask, "Hi, did you find everything you were looking for?"

I think I found some really bad grammar, but I reply, "Actually, no, I'm looking for date-nut bread."

"Date night bread?"

"No, date-nut bread." Is my New Yawk accent that terrible?

"Date night bread."

I sigh. Is this a comedy routine in which I must shout out 'third-base'?

"Date-nut dates with fruit and nuts, like this conversation. If there is such a thing as date night bread in the Sunshine State, then we are starting new traditions.

I'm starting to get a facial tic. "Okay, let's analyze this. At the annual state fair, everything is deep-fried from Twinkies to pickles. Next offering is macaroni and cheese on a burger hidden inside a glazed doughnut. But wait! The fair also offers what I have labeled "The Widow Maker." It's a pound of deep-fried bacon on a stick. I would not be surprised if the good citizens of Florida have produced date night bread. But that is not what I want"

As I finish my monologue, I realize the poor cashier is near tears. I offer consolation, "I'm sorry, my dear. You see, date-nut bread is really tasty and addictive. Now I may have to learn to bake it myself."

Looking at her name tag, I continue, "But I promise you, Amelia, next time I am up in the Big Apple I will buy quite a few loaves of date-nut bread and bring one to you."

Amelia's face brightens up. "Apples? We have apples. They're not really big, but they are very good for baking!"

Oy vey! Or, as they say in my old neighborhood, "You're freakin' kiddin' me, right?

* Please note: this is only my opinion and my digestive system's preference. You may or may not agree. I apologize but still stand firm on the foods I like.

HERE & NOW
Ginny Smythe

He spots her across the music cafe. She is swaying gently to the piped-in music. *What song is this?*

...you know it feels good to be alive
I was alive, and I waited, waited...*
He catches her eye and gives her his best boyish smile. *She is beautiful.*

She looks to her left and to her right. *Me? Is he smiling at me?* Realizing the answer to her own question, she is instantly embarrassed he has caught her singing to herself. *I'm such a dork.* But, she takes a chance and slowly smiles back at him. *He is quite handsome.* It was just this morning she talked with her roommate about getting back out there and dating again. She recalls her friend's advice, "Be present. Take a chance." And here she is smiling at a stranger. *Aren't I brazen?*

He motions to her as if to say, can I join you? She nods approvingly. *Who am I?*

He gets up and tries to slowly saunter toward her. He wants to keep his cool. *Don't look too eager! Be cool, dude. Cool.*

She fusses with her bangs and throws her long hair over her shoulder. *Give this guy a chance!*

He reaches the table, and she gestures for him to sit. He opens his mouth to speak, but she raises her hand and gestures to him to wait just a moment. She is still deeply involved with the song on the distant speaker.

"Here comes the chorus," she says.

I was alive, and I waited for this
Right here, right now
There is no other place I want to be
Right here, right now
Watching the world wake up from history

Realizing he might not wait for the end of the song, she suddenly asks, "What's your name?"

"I'm Here. What's your name?"

"I'm *here?*" she asks. "Of course you are, but what is your name?"

"Here," he retorts.

"What?" She begins to wish she hadn't encouraged him.

"Here. H-E-R-E, Here!" his voice reverberates.

"Your name is … Here?" she asks.

"Yes, my name is Here. Now, what is your name?" he challenges.

"My name is Now," she replies.

"Oh, I see…so, you are making fun of me because my name is Here. You're saying your name is Now. Or is it Then? Come on. Is Now really your name? What would even be the origin of that name?" he queries.

"Origin? There's no origin. Now really is my name," she says.

"How do you spell it?" he gives her a puzzled look.

"N. O. W. How do you think I spell it?" *He's making*

fun of my name. This guy is so rude. "Wait a minute! A guy named Here is making fun of *my* name?"

"Sorry, I didn't mean…but you have to admit it's a bit weird," he rallies.

"What's weird? That a girl could be named Now? My parents were musicians and were living in a van when I was born. "Hippies through and through," she admits and grins sheepishly.

"My parents were hippies too! I mean, my name is Here. That's not like being named Bill or Joe." he smiles back at her. "What's weird though is that my name is Here and your name is Now. You know, "Here and Now." He pauses, "Not to mention we met during the song "Right Here, Right Now." Now, That *is* weird, Now."

"That's not weird, Here. That's Lucky," she smiles coyly.

"Uh-huh, umm, urr," he stammers. "Mm-mmm… You're really not going to believe this, Now. But, Lucky? That's my dog's name!"

"Okay, then it's…Destiny," she smiles.

"Destiny? Destiny is…Destiny is my grandmother's name," he grins.

They both sit in comfortable silence gazing at each other and absorbing the last five minutes and the many coincidences.

And then, he takes a gulp, "Do you hear that, Now?"

"Hear what, Here?" she asks him.

"The song? Do you hear it?" Here blushes.
Now blushes too as she recognizes the melodious voice of Elvis singing, "Can't Help Falling in Love."

*Edwards, Mike. (1990). *"Right Here, Right Now."* On Right Here, Right Now by Jesus Jones. London: Matrix Studios. September 11.

THE NEW CAR
Dottie Littlefield

My nephew, Bob, told me about the family's new
car. He said he was trying to get his wife, Pam, to buy a
new car for months, but she kept putting it off because
she liked her old one. They were going to Pam's cousins farmhouse to spend the Thanksgiving Holiday. It's a
three- hour drive from where they live in Atlanta. Pam
was going to drive there two days earlier to help her
cousin get things ready for all the company.

Bob finally convinced Pam her old car wasn't safe to
drive that distance, and it would cost too much to fix
everything. So, they bought a new Lexus and traded in
the old one. She drove it to the farm on the Monday before Thanksgiving and called Bob to say it was a pleasure
to drive, but it made a small rattling noise that needed
to be checked. Bob drove there in his car with his two
daughters after they arrived home from college on Tues-
day night.

Wednesday morning, Dave, Judy's husband, and Bob
decided to play golf about thirty minutes away from the
farm. Pam asked Bob to drive their new car, so he could
check it out. Bob was happy to get a chance to drive it.
As they get in the car, Dave remarks how nice it is, and
Bob proudly agrees. He told Dave it took months to con-

vince Pam to get a new car. They hear a loud BEEP. They look at each other, and Bob asks, "What was that?"

Dave says, "I have no idea." He takes off his hat and tosses it in the back seat. BEEP.

As they drive away, they both chuckle and Bob says, "I guess I need to learn more about our new car." He checks the gauges to make sure everything is OK and BEEP it goes off again.

Bob asks Dave to check his seat belt, and he does, and says, "No it's not my seat belt." BEEP.

"Dave, please get the owner's manual out of the glove compartment and see if you can find – BEEP- anything that would explain what's wrong."

As Bob continues to drive, Dave looks through the manual and shakes his head. "There's nothing in here that -BEEP- explains what's making the beep."

Bob frantically checks all the gauges again, hoping he didn't miss anything that would ruin the car. BEEP. He asks, "You have a Lexus. Have you ever heard anything like this?"

"No. I haven't, but the sound is sort of familiar." BEEP.

Bob is frustrated and angry from listening to the BEEP every half-mile, and called Pam on his cell phone and asked if she knows what it is making the beep sound.

She replied, "I didn't have that problem driving the car. I just heard a rattle, and no one else has driven the car since I came here." BEEP

Bob called the dealership and complained to the salesman who sold him the car. "The new car is making a beeping sound as I drive it down the road."

The salesman says, "That's odd. -BEEP- I have never heard of anything like that. I will check with the service department right now."

They are put on hold -BEEP- and wait for the sales-man to come back online.

"Sir, no one in the service department has any idea what is causing the beep. Please bring the car in to be checked as soon as you can." BEEP.

"Did you hear that? It's really bad. BEEP. I can't imag-ine asking my wife to drive this car for three hours having to listen to it beep every half mile or so." BEEP.

The salesman apologized, but by this time, Bob was so angry he lost control. BEEP. He shouted,

"I want my old car back! Get all the paperwork ready to turn back around! I will not be stuck with this -BEEP- car making this sound."

He hung up as they finally arrive at the golf course. Bob is steaming angry and knows it's not going to be a fun day of golf.

Dave opens the rear passenger door to get his hat he had tossed in the backseat and asks, "What is this?" He lifts out a little round disk laying on the floor of the back-seat. Puzzled, they look at each other trying to figure out what it is and hear it beep.

Bob called Pam and asked, "Did you put something on the floor of the backseat of the car?"

"No. Judy, did you put something on the floor in the backseat of my car?"

"Oh yes, the smoke alarm needed a new battery, so I put it on the floor in the backseat of your car so we would remember to get a new battery. I thought we would be taking your car."

ROCK CHRONICLES I: FAMILY REUNION
Shanda Whittle

A purple haze hung low over the Hudson Valley, in the village of Woodstock, New York. A thin African American man sat strumming a guitar outside a tea shop. A black Western cowboy hat with a purple band and silver conchos rested low over his eyes to block out the sun. A psychedelically designed wind chime hung on the porch of the shop. It tinkled in the wind, and he tried to keep rhythm with it. The wind calmed, and the chimes stopped altogether when a big yellow taxi pulled up. A foxy lady in bell-bottom jeans, a denim shirt, a tan suede vest with beaded fringe, and large tinted glasses exited the cab in a cloud of ganga smoke.

"I'm lookin' for an old dairy farm around here," she told the man in a deep Southern accent, her hair disheveled and hanging down over her bloodshot eyes. "There was a groovy music and love festival there a couple years ago." The man kept strumming as the driverless taxi drove away, not raising his hat to look at the lady. He was bored with all the tourists looking to experience Woodstock. He was 26 when he played there and 27 when he died. Woodstock was an experience he remembered well. He lives here with his memories in a 76-year-old body that hasn't shown signs of aging after the age of 27.

Parents bring their children to town on family vacations looking to visit the iconic farm where Woodstock took place. Their children are embarrassed by their parents' hippie paraphernalia and try to overcome their boredom listening to modern-day music on their smartphones. Jimi had no intention of sticking around to entertain the lady or her family, wherever they were.

"Sorry, ma'am. The festival you're looking for happened almost 50 years ago. I'm afraid you're too late," he said, still not looking up at her. He stopped strumming his guitar, tipped his hat back to the top of his head, and got up to leave. "Enjoy your vacation, lady," he said as he walked away, not making eye contact with her.

The woman, startled by his familiar face, took a harmonica out of the pocket of her denim shirt. She blew a few tunes then sang, "I want you to come on, come on, come on, take another little piece of my heart now, baby." The man stopped in his tracks, and she waited, knowing he'd respond in turn. He always has, ever since they first met at the Monterey Pop Festival in '67.

He pushed his hat off the back of his head; the string hung around his neck. He turned to look at the woman and could barely believe his eyes when he saw the huge smile on Pearl's face. Her expression was equally surprised. He took the left-handed modified Fender Stratocaster he had hung over his shoulder and began to play, slowly walking toward her, crouching low while singing, "There must be some kind of way outta here. Said the joker to the thief. There's too much confusion. I can't get no relief." By this time her arms were raised in the air, and her body was movin' and groovin' to the song along with the beaded fringe of her suede vest.

Jimi Hendrix stood in front of Janis Joplin and stopped playing as he smiled and thought: is it possible I'm looking at a dear friend I lost so many years ago? He looked over Janis's plump face with her trouble-making grin.

"Is that really you Pearl?" he asked with trepidation and disbelief.

Her smile grew bigger, and her arms reached out and grabbed him in a tight hug. "It's me, baby. It's me!" He had been sentenced to a life, living among the ruins of Overlook Mountain, above Woodstock, New York for all eternity. Was it possible a dear friend and fellow blues-rock musician had come to join him? He had read about his death nearly 50 years ago in London and heard that Janis had overdosed on heroin in Hollywood less than a month later. Not quite Romeo and Juliet, but close.

He wrote the song, "Castles Made of Sand" in '67, the same year he met Janis at the Monterey Pop Festival. Some said the lyrics spoke of his tumultuous childhood with an alcoholic father, domestic abuse between his parents, and his family being torn apart in many ways.

On September 18, 1970, Jimi's castle made of sand slipped into the sea where he knew it eventually would come to be. Those few that truly knew him denied he committed suicide and believed he decided to exit when the circumstances were right. After his soul slipped away from his mortal life, he found himself atop Over-look Mountain observing the hilly farm fields where he played the closing performance of the three-day festival of music, peace, and love. If he had been here for almost 49 years, where had Pearl been? The two had a lot of catching up to do. He threw his arm around her, and the two started walking toward Overlook Mountain, giddily sharing stories accumulated from the five decades since their deaths.

MY HAT
Shelley Leiman

I have been shot by little cowboys with their finger pistols. I have been asked, "Where is your horse?" But oddly enough, until now, no one has asked me why I wear a cowboy hat wherever I go. This question has now begun to consume me. Why do I? What possible reasons have I hidden from myself? Must I uncover forgotten moments in my past that have influenced me, forcing me to perform self-analysis of which I am incapable? Would it be productive, or would it create a stressful situation which might force me to seek a professional analyst? And let's be honest, who really cares about its origins! Actually, the question is flawed. It could be construed as "When did you start to wear them" or rather "Why do you wear them now?" Perhaps I must approach both inquiries, so no one will again pin me to the wall and shout, "But why?"

Hats have fascinated me since I was a little kid. Our family cats endowed us with several litters of kittens, and my greatest pleasure was to dress them in my dolls' clothes, bonnets and all, and force the poor squealing toys to remain in my doll carriage. (This occurred long before Dr. Seuss). As I grew older, my siblings and I made our own costumes and headgear for family enter-tainment. We were such hams. Only our family could survive our skits.

My mother used to tell me I was an inquisitive child, questioning most everything I was told. When I had learned to sew, my dearest friend and I shocked our fellow students by creating and wearing homemade one-armed shirts and loud, plaid, pedal pushers. Was this rebellion, a symptom of self-expression and exploration as we defied the impulse to fit into cultural norms? Why do people smile and say, "I like your hat"! I think as they accept me, they see the courage and feelings of happiness on my face.

Today I have a collection of many hats, ranging from delicate feminine styles to Russian furs with ear flaps, a Victorian hat I recently created for an amateur drama production, and others, hanging on my bedroom wall, waiting to be worn on special occasions. But I will never forget the day I found the hat of my life, a straw Western job. The moment I saw it on the counter at Dillard's, I tried it on and looked in the mirror. I could not help but smile. I really, really liked it. It had a panache I couldn't define and gave me an inner joy I couldn't deny. I was a child again. I was a cowgirl! I couldn't resist buying it. My husband looked at me and said, "I like that hat! It looks great; buy it!" and so I did, and I found myself wearing it day after day, wherever we went.

I did not intend it to become a sort of trademark or even an attraction, but it did, and more. Wherever I wore it, I was greeted by old people, young ones, male and female, people from many different cultures, and always with a smile as they said "I like your hat!" It became a sort of mantra. Many people said it, but I felt it. My chronic social shyness morphed into joy. I felt confident and protected. "I like your hat" seemed to be a mantra that opened up a different dimension of life for me. Western hats came to my rescue when I felt alone or frightened or reclusive. And they still do.

People have worn hats for many reasons; for protection, cultural conformation, tradition, etc. I have accepted the view that the Western-style I wear has given me a feeling of sheer joy and well-being. But that's me! I am so glad that in today's society, more and more people find their lives are enhanced by expressing their individualism and being encouraged by their fellow human beings. That's how I feel. Try it. You'll like it.

And now when I wear my hat, I remember what my husband said to me whenever we were out shopping, "It's okay, you go along, and I'll catch up with you. As long as you wear your hat, I'll find you." Now, as I peer beneath the brim of my Western hat, I don't feel alone and afraid.

LIFE WITH MY FUR BABIES
Judith Ann Pelio

I'd been searching for more than six months, looking at every online animal rescue site in Palm Beach County. There was always a reason why I thought, not this one, maybe that one, this one for sure, but what about the one with three legs? I should not be looking for another dog; I already had three! But, deep inside my heart, I knew there was one particular dog that was crying out for help, my help.

I volunteered many hours at a local animal rescue facility and fell in love with every dog I saw; big dogs, small dogs, adult or puppy. I loved them all. Volunteering at an animal rescue facility was hard work. There was always a kennel to clean and line with paper, water and food dishes to fill, and towels and blankets to be washed. Throughout the day, there always were garbage bags that needed to be thrown into the dumpster. And, the dogs needed playtime, walk time, and time to relax and sleep.

Every day we took the dogs from their kennels and put them in the front of the rescue where they could be seen by passersby. I could pick them up and hold them like babies or play with them if they were large dogs. People came into the facility and picked up the dogs, held them, and talked to them. But, usually, they just needed their puppy fix for the day and left without adopting a dog. That always felt so sad to me, watching someone leave without adopting one of the dogs. Looking at these dogs, I felt they had similar feelings.

One weekend, a busload of puppies was picked up by van from an overcrowded rescue in north Florida. They arrived at the rescue in south Florida, where I was volunteering. I immediately fell in love with two, fat, little puppies of mixed origin. They were siblings; one was named Helen, and the other was Harrison. Within a week, I wanted to foster the puppies. They were a real challenge to train and keep from biting anything on which they could put their baby teeth. I, too, had a biting problem because every time I looked at the puppies, I had to pick them up and bite their fat, little bellies.

After fostering the puppies, going through their spaying and neutering, I was in love with them and decided on adoption. I bought them name tags, outfits, and toys. They had separate beds but always slept together. They were the cutest puppies I had ever seen. I changed Helen's name to Princess Grace, and Harrison became Prince Harry. I loved them fiercely even when they peed and pooped wherever and whenever it was convenient for them to do so. They put their front paws on the pee-pee pads then peed on the floor. Training them would be a minor challenge, but certainly not a problem.

Finally, after almost two months fostering them, I completed the necessary paperwork to adopt my Princess Grace and Prince Harry. Soon, I would give them their forever homes where I could hug and love them and bite their bellies for the rest of their lives. I submitted the adoption package to the rescue facility where I volunteered. I was blissful with anticipation and excitement.

The next morning, while I waited to hear about the adoption, I received a picture from the Humane Society of Highland Falls in Sebring, FL, some three to four hours from my home. The image was of a small Chihuahua looking into a camera with traumatized eyes. As I looked into her eyes, I wondered what had happened to cause that kind of fear. Had she been abused? Was she from a dog mill where she was there just for breeding? Was she from a home where she was unwanted and abused? What was the troublesome story behind those eyes?

I called the Sebring Humane Society to inquire about Dog #11725, named Bella Jean. They told me that the dog was dropped off at their facility two days ago because the owners no longer wanted her. She was no older than a year and a half; yet, she already had a litter of puppies. She weighed less than five pounds. The facility advised me that they would answer questions if I wanted to visit them to meet the dog. I said I'd be there in three and a half to four hours, depending on traffic. I asked myself why would I drive so far because of one dog out of the hundreds I had seen on other websites within ten to twenty minutes from my house? Why this dog? What was it I had seen in her eyes that led to an impromptu decision to drive some eight hours round trip to see her? As I drove to Sebring, I kept asking myself, "Why."

Almost four hours later, I arrived at the Humane Society to visit Dog #11725, Bella Jean. As soon as I told
the front desk who I was there to see, they asked me if I
knew that she was very skittish. I said I assumed she was
traumatized at some point. There was only one person at
the entire facility who could touch Bella Jean. That person would introduce the dog to me. I sat on the floor as
she was escorted from her kennel to meet me. She was
so terrorized by anyone who attempted to touch her. She
screeched and ran to the other end of a very large room
where there was a door. She wanted to disappear behind
it. The sounds coming from this dog were pitiful, and she
wailed with intense fear and terror. No one could get
within ten feet of her without her running away, screech-
ing, and acting terrified. My thought was to leave without her and concentrate on the two puppies I planned to
adopt. Also, why would I take a dog that I couldn't get
near, couldn't touch, and couldn't hold? What would I
do with her once we got home? How would she react
to the puppies and my three other fur babies? Suddenly,
I heard myself requesting that Bella Jean be placed in
my dog carrier and set on the front seat of my car. I was
going home, and Bella Jean was coming with me!

For the next two days, Bella Jean (now Baby Rose,)
would not come out of the carrier. I put pee-pee pads,
water, and food in the kennel and carried it wherever I
went. I spoke to her softly, told her I loved her, and continuously tried to get her approval. She went to the back
of the kennel and trembled each time I opened the door.

When I went to bed, I put the kennel on a chair right next to my bed so that I could put my fingers through the holes to let Baby Rose know that I would not hurt her. She sniffed at my fingers and returned to the rear of the kennel. During the day, I placed the kennel on the floor so the puppies (whom I was waiting to adopt) and my three other babies could exchange some sniffs. By day three, I decided to take Baby Rose out of the kennel even if she wanted to bite me. I reached into the kennel, and she shook as I picked her up. I spoke softly to calm her terror. I knew then that Baby Rose would never, ever be hurt again. It was then that I also knew why we bonded. We had something in common, the terror, the fear, and the paralyzing concern of being hurt again. She was learning to trust me without the intense fear that I would hurt her. So, my fur babies were six in total. This is why God put me on this earth.

The following day, I received an email from the rescue where I was fostering the puppies. They stated that my Homeowner's Association had a limit on the number of dogs permitted at each home. I was devastated and frantically called the rescue to tell them there was no such limit in the Development's By-Laws. I called everyone I knew at the animal rescue and left messages asking that they give me the opportunity to prove there was no such limit on the number of dogs one could have. I pleaded with them to adopt the puppies whom I had for close to two months. No one returned my numerous calls. I returned the puppies to the rescue, and they were adopted the following day. I don't know who rescued them, where the family lived, or if they kept the name tags I had made for the puppies. I felt empty, devastated, and personally betrayed. I never went back to volunteer at that animal rescue.

For the next couple of weeks, I cried almost continuously. Where were the puppies? Who adopted them? Were they happy? Did they get loving, forever homes? I looked at their pictures on the rescue's website every day until their beautiful, puppy faces were taken down. They were someone else's babies now, and I would never get to hold them or kiss them or bite their little bellies again. I would never know who they were with and how they were treated. I lost them unjustly and would have to live with that loss. I felt so deceived and manipulated by the very rescue I had given so much effort, time, and love.

To this day, some six months later, I still cry for the puppies. I see the holes they dug in the grass, the chewed parts of the kitchen mat, the baby pen where they stayed overnight in their beds. I remember the day they were spayed and neutered. I remember crying because they cried and how I held them until they fell asleep. I remember sleeping on the floor inside their baby gate to help them relax after their surgeries. I remember their dishes, beds, outfits, and toys. They brought so much joy into my life. Then, suddenly, they were gone and no longer mine. I still grieve for them. There are evenings when I go to bed crying that they are not in my bed. I wonder if they are happy in someone else's bed, someone else's lap, someone else's arms. I pray that they are happy and being treated well. I pray also that, by some miracle, I will see them again. Oh, God, how much my heart hurts!

* * * * *

Yet, through all the pain and anguish, I am so grateful that Baby Rose is mine and she is learning to trust me. We have a long way to go, but we are taking baby steps to get there. She had once cried out for help and, because of what I saw in her eyes, she got the help, my help. Again, I am reminded of why God put me on this earth.

UNEXPECTED ARRIVAL

Margie Bonner

It was February, still winter, and I had just turned 17. I had been working for about six months and making my own money. I felt grown up. My family was a large one, and we had been taught early, to care for ourselves and to provide for ourselves.

My job entailed caring for a family's children while the parents worked. I lived with the family, as my home was about 30 miles away. I had weekends off, and took the train home on Friday night and returned back on Sunday evening.

I felt very mature. I was entrusted with three children, the youngest nine months old. I took care of the house, doing all the things a mother would do. I was very thankful for the fact that I was used to babies and young children. My three older sisters had children, and often times they visited. It all seemed easy to me, and I remember enjoying the days.

I needed a winter coat, one that was full length. People of importance wore them. Women bustling up and down the streets, carrying what looked like briefcases. I wanted to look like them and to feel like a woman of substance. I was now earning my own spending money and decided to splurge on what I desired, which was a new full- length winter coat. It took weeks of trying on coats. I weighed a whopping ninety pounds, and most coats engulfed me. I was not to be detoured from my quest. I was determined to buy a ladies coat and to look good in it. Finally, I found it. I remember looking into the full-length mirror. I saw a thin young girl with big eyes and a serious expression. That was me. I was meant to have it. The color was light gray tweed with flecks of yellow. The coat had a rolled collar with a large gold button that held the coat closed. Best of all, I felt sophisticated, no more, was I going to be taken for a kid. Wow! What a feeling.

The very next weekend, I traveled home. My new coat felt warm and snug, and so far was everything I had hoped for. I left the train station and made my way down the street to meet up with my brother and friends. My home town was built on a hill. I started the walk full of purpose and confidence. The sidewalk was crowded, which was usual for a Friday night. I surveyed the street ahead and felt nothing but satisfaction.

Suddenly without warning, both feet slipped out from under me, and I fell completely down, landing on my back. Worst of all, I began to slide faster and faster. Suddenly I was flying down that sidewalk as if I was on a sled. I could literally feel my dignity trailing along behind me. Shattered, torn, never to be regained. I felt frantic. The coat I had chosen so carefully was woolen, making it as slippery as if it had been waxed. Thoughts flew through my head, I looked about, to my dismay I saw boots move out of my way, ladies shoes moved away as if making a path for me. I needed help, yet none was offered. I managed to turn enough on my side to see a snowbank that lined the edge of the sidewalk. I turned even more and came to rest against the bank. With all the finesse I could manage, I got to my feet.

I felt my face flush, yet I made no eye contact. I brushed the snow from my coat and with legs that trembled I made my way to the destination I had planned. I spoke not a word about this incident, and as I remember, no one remarked on my new coat. One may wonder what I did with the coat, as far as I can recall, my old familiar jacket felt fine for the rest of the winter. The coat was laid to rest as well as my dreams of being a woman of substance.

MAN ON THE STREET
Hartley Barnes

I am speaking to all of you sitting in front of me. This story is about me. Do not believe me if you think everyone should be like you. It was an experience I created in an attempt to find the one thing missing from my life. Do not believe me if you think I am joking.

I woke up somewhere this morning; I am not sure where but somewhere. It is just another morning. It does not matter where I am or what day it is. After all these months, I am still not comfortable with the morning chill. I wait eagerly for the sun to appear and Cover me with its blanket until I am warm while seeking breakfast. What will it be today? Depends on the various cans along the way, choices are not a luxury; neither are the events of the day. One thing is sure; many faces will stare me down and scowl at the stench that is a part of me. I won't acknowledge them, but I will ask myself what else are they thinking.

I am thoroughly engrossed in my situation and refuse to feel regretful. It is not pathetic in my mind as it is in yours. Of course, that is speculation on my part; after all, if I could read your thoughts, I would be super rich and famous and looking down on the street people I am pretending to be.

So how did I get here? The guesses are numerous as to why; only one is imperative, mine. I made a commitment; this is not about a sad life. It is about being happy. It is my choice to find what I am missing; it is not about the expectations of others. I carry that particular thought with me each day as I survive the streets; this thing is about me. Why am I out here? I reached a crossroads, and I made a decision to go up, down, right, left, wherever. Some will question my choice. Some may consider me insane, but this is about me. I have it all; I want for nothing, except for one major thing— happiness.

Can I sacrifice what is in the right hand for what could be in the left– happiness?

The common thread between all judges is knowledge or lack of it. I have never asked anyone to feel sorry for me, which would be a contradiction. I choose my present lifestyle because of what it could offer me. Happiness, with all the turmoil that surrounds me, contentment. Can I find it in the most unexpected place?

Judges of all types, the skeptics, the misguided compassionate, Doctors, and those rotten human beings, say, "He is troubled," without ever asking me a single question. I trudge through each day, not knowing who or what I will encounter. One thing is sure: life is a bitch!

A young woman walking her dog, and just before she passed me the dog deviated, pulling her toward me. The dog smells my leg, sneezes and looks up at me as if to say, "Good day, sir! How are you? I am sorry people do not understand your circumstances." The woman yanked the leash, "Bad dog, bad dog!" I saw her again without the dog, and she said, "How are you today, sir?"

I replied. "If I were any better, I would be twins." The young lady's dog thought her a lesson. You may think that is uncommon; it is not; children have taught their parents the same lesson.

Put me in a frame and try to decipher the nuances you see and there will be a wide range of interpretations. Connotations base on first impressions, preconceived ideas, and the stigma you think I represent. The question I should be asking is, why, why is it so difficult for you to fathom that I want to be on the streets? I know you do not understand why so you assume. Why not just ask me? The answer might astound you.

At times I have to admit I deliberately do something unusual to get a reaction, and depending on where I am, I try to guess the answers I will get. I call it geograph-ic responses, for instance, I am in an affluent area, and someone will alert the police. I pretended to be a bark-ing dog, and of course, the cops showed up. By then, all the dogs in the area could hear me barking, and started barking themselves.

"Sir, I am responding to several calls about you bark-ing and disturbing the peace," said the cop.

"No! My dog was yelping. I will try to keep him qui-et."

"Where is he?"

"He just ran off, going to do his thing, he'll be back."

"You don't belong in this neighborhood."

"Is this a street?"

"Yes, sir."

"Then this is my home."

"You don't belong here."

"This is my home."

"Where do you live, sir?"

"Anywhere I am."

"When your dog gets back you, and he leaves this neighborhood or I will be forced to arrest both of you for disturbing the peace."

I do not think he realized what he said — arresting a dog! Is he going to bust the other dogs as well? He did not patronize me.

"Officer, I appreciate your approach, thank you."

As I turned to walk off, he asked, "Are you going to be okay?"

"Yes, I live by faith, not hope."

"I don't understand," he said.

"Hope is not faith and faith is undeniable without reservation, so when I talk to God, I let him know I have no doubts. Yes, I will be okay. By the way, officer, I don't have a dog."

"I know," he said with such sympathy. "Be careful."

A little girl came up to me. In her hand, she had a dollar that she tried to give it to me, and I refused to take it. That was a wrong move on my part. She started to cry; I had hurt her feelings. She'd offered me the money as a gift from her heart, not out of pity; Whether or not I needed the dollar, I should have recognized her innocence. I was amazed by this child and disappointed in myself for my dearth of insight in the way I reacted to her.

For a moment I slipped into one of the crevices I go for self-protection, a place I should not be because I choose the street and nothing should cause me to question my self-worth.

Understandably, the child's father became upset. "Look what you did." Her father shouted.

"Sir, she's a reflection of you, can I talk to her? I can explain why I did not take her dollar."

"Yes." He replied.

"What is her name?"

"Rachel."

I got on my knees, "My name is Mr. Tony. I am so sorry I made you cry, Rachel. Can I tell you why I did not take your dollar?"

"Yes," she said as her father handed her a tissue.

"I'm pretending to be someone I'm not," I said.

"Why, you don't like yourself?"

"I do very much, you see, Rachel, I am pretending to be someone I am not because I am trying to find something I don't have ..."

"Your family?" she asked.

"No. I'm trying to find happiness."

"I'll give you some of mine."

"Thank you, but I have to search for it. Do you think you could give your dollar to someone who needs it? I bet your Dad can help you find such a person?"

"Okay, I forgive you." My heart melted, hearing those words.

It was raining, so I sought cover under the canopy of a boutique; after a couple of minutes, the owner came out.

"Go somewhere else! You are stopping my clients from coming in; you cost me money."

"Don't you think the rain has something to do with that? How many customers did you have before I got here?"

"That is not relevant." She hissed.

"Don't you see it's raining?"

"What I see is in front of me, and is not important, leave, or I will call the authorities."

When am I looked at what do you see, psychopath, schizophrenia, the trash that nobody wants, or potential going down the drain? What, what do you see? In what category are you putting me? Those are questions from the honesty quiz to question self, what do you see and why? Do not be ashamed; you are not alone. I understand that it is in your nature to leap before you look.

Is the glass half full or is the glass half empty, I know it's not very original, but it serves the purpose, who are you? I dare to be me, who are you? Are you qualified to admonish me, to be my juror and ignorant of the facts? Who are you? You must live in my situation to know me; what you see is not always so. Who are you?

A very older woman I had a conversation with, said,

"Times change, I am time. I have lived many decades, do you think your circumstances are any different from mine now that I have aged. Time goes on but will stop for me. The family will gather to pay respect. One selected to read the eulogy, to big me up but will fail to mention how forgotten I am. Placed in a place, I do not want to be. Occasionally visited to satisfy one's consciences and the thinking propagated to the next generation and the and following, and the following. You set aside the one that brought you into this world, the one that is now an encumbrance and move on till it's your turn.

I said to her, unhappily, "You don't have a choice, I do." She looked at me, scratched her head, and walked off.

My journey is never-ending as long I can breathe, how long it will be I can not say and is not an issue for me, it is what it is, I am in pursuit of bliss. In the meantime, I will continue to ride the waves as I guide my destiny in a temporary world.

I recall walking on the campus of a prestigious university. I stopped to listen to a professor lecturing his class about human tragedy under a tree. Even though there were eyes on me, I stayed and heard, and I waited for the students to leave.

"Where did you get your information from?" I asked the professor.

"Books," he said. Cut and dried, just books.

"The real story is on the streets, not on paper; spend some time on the streets. People who have no inkling as to why a man or a woman ends up on the streets. Is it by choice? Was it supposed to be temporary, was there no other option? Do they have a damn reason? In books, you can't see the eyes that will speak to you, that express pain, desolation, isolation, scorn, and peace of mind."

He was upset, but he understood what I said. Facts bring about understanding; street people need to be unwritten. Do not tell their story based on your perception and the perception of others. Come and live it with them. The script should be honest.

I set no limits. Do not place any on me. I too have a responsibility regardless of my ideology, not to disrupt the ongoing of everyday life. I am not dropping out; I am just living for me. Do not tell me about political correctness; there is no value in it. If my intentions misconstrued, maybe it is time to reflect on you.

Several women stop to talk to me. Well, not exactly. One of them asked me, "Do you bathe?"

"No!" Another one said. "The shock of the water will kill him!"

"I would not want to be like him, do you think he knows where he is?"

Those kinds of questions amuse me.

There is an automatic supercilious idea that the people, meaning, street people, are an affliction on society. Why? They are not productive. There is some truth to that. We do not pay taxes. Agreed, let me separate myself for a second. How many working people do you know that don't pay taxes? Moreover, they are the majority. Think about some of the other things they do not do. Think! Think! I am back in the mix now. I heard you loud and clear. Why did I separate myself for a moment? THINK!

Recently I spoke to a politician who was running for office, his platform was saving the homeless, and my question to him was, "What makes you think street people want to be saved?"

"You mean homeless people."

"No sir, street people, the street is their home, so they are not homeless."

He seemed a little confused. I reiterated my question.

"Well, we must be sympathetic to those who cannot take care of themselves, who have lost the courage to live like normal people. We, as outstanding and upright citizens of this free country, must take care of those who have tuned out and cannot recover. Elect me, and I will introduce legislation to have those people removed from the streets and placed where they belong!"

I did not vote for him, not because he was condescending; because he was just a. You fill in the blanks!

It was a cold day, and I love gospel music, so I passed a church, and I could hear the choir singing, their voices permeated the cold air, and hit me with such warmth. I decided to go into the church and listen. As I entered through the door, I am stopped and scrutinized. An elder guarding the entrance said to me, "This is the house of God. I don't think the flock, including myself, wants you here."

"Am I not a child of God?"

"Yes," the elder said," but you don't fit in; God's people are clean and decent."

That was a fascinating answer. I said, "Thank you. I
will listen from outside."

As I listened, I thought that man could only be speaking for himself. I went back to the church, passed him
before he could stop me, and took a seat. The woman
next to me handed me a Bible. I opened the Bible, and
by coincidence, the page I opened to was Mark 12:31.
"Love your neighbor as yourself."

I am back to where I started. On the streets, I found
another set of rules, another community that is chastised
based on appearance and not substance; people rele-
gated to the well of despair.

I did not find what is missing.

I CRIED FOR US

Karina G. Felix

I cried because of what I saw in your soul when our eyes first connected.

I saw a mirror image of me. I saw the hurt, the abandonment and the sad side that no one ever sees.

I saw our need for love and acceptance: Our need for acknowledgement and appreciation, a need to not hide anymore.

I saw a need for a confidant, a partner, a soul mate. We don't have the need to talk because we see each other. Really see.

You looked into me, and I looked into you. Our vision bypassed the exterior and permeated deep into the interior of our soul and spirit.

I long to know you better; yet I hesitate, lest I drive you away.

I will patiently wait for you. I know what I know and, hopefully, you know too.

I cried for us: our hearts so tender. The children we once were.

Can we still save them, protect them, and let them know that they will be fine?

We will take care of them because we're the only people they trust.

The children we once were will understand that all is well.
Our souls are whole and our hearts are healed.

I cried for the children we were.

I cried for us.

UNFORGETABLE

Virginia Guido

Giggling, gossiping, and ghost stories were the norm of Lena's pajama parties; but after one specific night, those girls would forever sleep with one eye open.

They sat cross-legged in a circle with Lena holding a flashlight. She dimmed the bedroom lights and positioned the beam under her chin, appearing ghostlike. "Listen up," she whispered, "this house is truly haunted. There's a presence here. Can you feel it? No? Not yet? Be still, listen, and maybe you 'll hear it."

A bouncing sound emanated from the ceiling; in the corner of the room. It didn't sound like a rubber ball, but an old fashion wooden ball.

"Who's doing that?" asked Maria, "is that your brother upstairs?"

"No, not my brother, but I have an idea." Lena aimed the flashlight at the ceiling. "It's always in that spot about this time every night. So I did a little research on the history of this house.

"Let's go upstairs; the room is empty right now. Mom's last boarder didn't stay long — maybe a week. Nobody lasts in that room for very long."

The girls followed Lena as she climbed up the stairs of the brownstone and tiptoed into the vacant furnished room. Lena panned the flashlight over the room, creating dancing shadows on every surface. It was eerily silent,

Lena continued her story

"This house is almost 200 years old. Entire families would reside here and raise their kids; cousins, uncles, aunts, everyone under one roof. They all lived, died, and were waked in this house. You saw the cut out in the wall at the top of the stairs, right? That was so the corner of the coffin would not hit the wall as it was carried down to the street.

"People weren't so healthy back then, and some died at a very young age younger than we are. There was a little boy about seven years old who used to play with a wooden ball. He would roll it into blocks like a bowling ball, toss it in the air and catch it, or spin it around his other toys. He always had that ball with him. It was his favorite plaything. One year, after a bad winter, he caught pneumonia and was confined to his bed until the end of his life

"Knowing he wasn't going to survive, he asked his mom to bury his ball with him. Through her tears, she promised him. He smiled as he took his last breath. At that moment, his small hand slipped off the bed and released the ball he was clutching. It hit the floor with the thud, continued to bounce itself out, then rolled away. The boy's mom searched but never found her son's favorite toy."

Lena took a breath for dramatic effect. "That poor boy was laid to rest without the wooden ball he loved." Lena's friends were wide-eyed and speechless, afraid to move or look around the room. They focused their attention on Lena. She was not finished.

"So every night, at about this time I hear the sound of a wooden ball hitting the floor and bouncing itself out." Lena looked around at the girls and shrugged.

"Are you putting us on?" Jen sounded doubtful.

"No, I'm serious." I wanted to show you what's going on here. No one rents this place or stays long when they do. As her flashlight flickered and died, a glowing mist formed by the bed. Even Lena was alarmed by the sight.

From the mist, a soft, childlike voice eerily addressed the group. "She's telling the truth, you know. And it happened in this very room."

CROSS ROADS
John F. Rifenberg

Dear God or "Higher Power": I said "higher power." That's for all my friends with addiction problems, which means all of my friends.

God, I know this is your busy season, so I really hate to bother you. But I have a problem understanding the whole Easter thing. I've seen almost all the faith laden and inspirational movies about this holiday. This is your only Son you sacrificed. Just how do we show respect, with a holiday that features an Easter bunny and other sweet candy? I just don't get the connection, the tragedy of the whole story. The real story is so different than the movies, aside from the "Ten Commandments" and of course, the Good Book needs to be read by everyone, including myself. So what happened? How did it end up this commercial sales bonanza? Where did all the thinking go wrong? I hate to bring this up again; I know it's your busy season, but what about the Buffalo Bills losing four straight Super Bowls...come on, God, what were you thinking? Thank you for your time. I know you are busy. And I also promise to be a good person, honest to G...sorry about that.

After my prayers that morning, I just happened to walk into a large national department store at the mall. The first and only thing I could see was Easter merchandise everywhere, just rows and rows for our Easter shopping pleasure. This is the holiday, for people who don't go to church; they go to church on this day. It's one of the big three of church days…Christmas Mass, Easter and of course the Super Bowl Sunday. Okay maybe four, Palm Sunday is a biggie too, because you get something for nothing…palms. Easter is special; after a long winter, it's a sign of spring. Not to mention, this is the weekend that we celebrate the killing of God's only Son, who rises from the dead and goes to heaven. After church, there's Easter Brunch with the whole family. Mother is wearing her new Easter dress and hat. Father, is wearing his new spring suit, making it an extra special day. All of this is set in stone just like the "Ten Commandments" unless the weatherman doesn't cooperate. Everyone is looking their Sunday best! Just what are we celebrating again?

The Easter Bunny, which could pass for an ordinary rabbit, doesn't lay eggs. They have little babies called kits or kittens. Just another strange twist in this Easter story, it's the chickens who supplied the eggs for the Easter Bunny. This morning starts before brunch is served when the children get to go on the annual Easter egg hunt. This is the hunt for eggs that they colored with their parents the night before. They color them with dyes that mom and dad bought for them. It's a family tradition. Obviously extra eggs are also brought. Everyone is an artist when it comes to coloring eggs. Naturally, the eggs have to be put into some kind of basket…like an Easter basket. Everyone gets to have their own personal basket, sometimes for years. Maybe the basket will be passed down to their children someday. It's almost a family tradition. The basket will also hold candy Easter bunnies and chocolate eggs and the favorite, candied little chicken bunnies. Who started all of this?

So, the story begins:

It was a warm, sunny day in spring. For the middle of the day, it was eerily quiet. The dusty and dirty road was lined with people dressed in robes to protect them from the intense spring sun. Some of the people were crying. Others were there just to have something to talk about and see the blood. A young man with long hair and beard was dragging a large wooden cross down the dirt road and up to the hill. His tattered clothes were covered with blood. The cries were growing louder as the man got closer to the top of the hill. It was a painful and hateful walk. Two more men were also there, petty thieves who were at the wrong place at the wrong time. Both of these poor souls were also dragging a wooden cross to the top of the hill. They couldn't believe the terrible sentence they were given for stealing. Usually, the courts just cut off a man's hand for stealing. Who, ever that man was, ahead of them on the dirt road, he sure made the courts angry. Now, all three of them were going to be dead within hours.

The first man, up the hill, who was surrounded by Roman soldiers, struggled with each step. The soldiers were keeping the peasants away from him, whether they wanted to help him or stone him. The Roman maidens tried to keep their children busy and away from the frightful scene. Each child was given eggs to color with special dyes. Each child got a color that was just his or hers to use. There were plenty of eggs to be had because the Christians had given up eggs for Lent.

In the midst of all of this, a white rabbit appeared from behind a stone building and ran across the road, tripping the young man making him crash to the ground with the cross on his back. Mayhem broke out, two of the Roman soldiers chased after the speedy rabbit, knowing the great flavor of a rabbit stew. Then an older woman slipped out of the crowd and started to give the man on the ground some water. A soldier pulled the woman away; another older man then tried to help the man with the heavy cross lying across his back. In the chaos, the old man slid a small package in the man's pocket. The soldier started to drag the old man away, but he tripped and fell on the young man with the cross. In that moment he whispered into the ear of the fallen man. "Its dark chocolate…it will give you energy."

The followers of the man were called "The Disciples" were sprinkled amongst the crowd. Some of them were crying for their "Master." Some of the others were looking for a Port-o-Potty, having lower track problems due to eating too much ham and sweet potatoes and drinking wine at the last supper. It was a long afternoon for everyone. Later that evening, everyone who was involved in this murder was a total basket case. Happy Easter!

THIS IS 40
Tajuana Troy

It was the summer of August 2017. My husband and I were living apart and on the verge of divorce, and my 40th birthday was coming up quickly. My 40th birthday was significant to me because I knew that by the time I turned 40 that the kids would be away at college, I would be closer to retirement, and there would be time for me to focus on myself.

My estranged husband decided that he would plan a trip to Jamaica because he knew how important my 40th birthday was to me. It also was a way for him to redeem himself and profess his love for me, HA! I guess you can say it was a new beginning to our relationship. Meanwhile, I was so excited about going to Negril, Jamaica, for the first time and … have I mentioned I was turning 40?

Let's rewind to six months before the vacation; the separation was due to my husband having an affair for the second time. Although separated, we decided not to give up and to work on the marriage. We attended marriage counseling for about five months, but it came to a halt when the therapist told me I should divorce my husband. He wasn't able to give me details due to confidentiality, but he told me my husband stopped attending his sessions.

In my heart, I knew I needed to let the marriage go,

but I was turning 40. I didn't want to start over, and I wanted answers about what was going on. I continued to go to therapy alone and work on my issues. I lost sleep torturing myself as I waited for answers from someone who didn't even love himself. I went along with his narcissistic, manipulative behavior while waiting for things to change. I searched for answers and didn't stop until I had a broken heart at 40.

Off I went on vacation to Jamaica with a man I once loved with all my heart but who now feels like a total stranger. We pretended to be happy when he picked me up at our home where he no longer resided. We strode through the airport pretending to be the perfect couple because it felt like the right thing to do, after all, it was my 40th birthday, and we were going to Jamaica. We were in full Hollywood character at the Cliff Hotel. It was perfect. I fell in love with the hotel so much that I forgot about my problems with him.

Our hotel room was decorated when I walked in. A large bouquet of my favorite red roses and a cold bottle of champagne sat next to the table with two glasses. An oversized "Happy Birthday" banner was posted on the wall just above the headboard and towels folded into swans adorned the bed. The balcony had an oversized hammock with a small table for two. It also had an excellent view facing the cliff and the ocean awaiting a beautiful sunset. The location was in walking distance of all of the local attractions. I thought to myself. I'm spending my 40th birthday in the best place imaginable with the absolute wrong person.

That evening we returned to the hotel after having a surprisingly enjoyable day out. I knew the marriage was over but my obsession over finding out what happened—what he did to me—came with me to Jamaica. I still wanted answers. I wanted to have proof to give myself a peace of mind what I got instead when I finally got those answers felt like a piece of HELL.

While he was in the shower, I took full advantage of his smartphone. Smartphones are not that smart because they don't lie. I went through his messages; it took only five minutes to find out what I needed to know. It hit me like a bullet train. My palms were sweating, my heart was racing, and I wanted to cry, but I couldn't show any signs of weakness. I took a deep breath and said, "Self, take time and figure out how you want this to play out."

We had dinner at the hotel restaurant right on the cliff. I tried to focus on the alluring sunset, the waves, and the sound of the ocean. It was so relaxing and nerve-wracking at the same time. I didn't want to ruin the moment, but I couldn't avoid reality. I processed in my head a thousand scenarios and their outcome, and I couldn't see any without me exploding. I let my thoughts keep processing as I tried to enjoy delightful Jamaica. I even had a specially prepared birthday meal by the chef.

It was so beautiful. How could I ruin this lovely occasion? I kept saying to myself. I was feeling so many emotions inside of me while I kept smiling and pretending throughout dinner. After dessert, we were relaxed and walked over to the edge of the cliff. As I looked out into the ocean, I thought about how I could get away with murder. I wanted to push him off that cliff for hurting me, but, I knew there would be consequences. I had to cancel that scene.

I took a different approach--I decided to make the moment intimate and started expressing my love for him. He began to relax and let me in a little, not knowing I was manipulating him. Then my questions about our relationship and marriage started coming rapidly. He seemed puzzled and defensive at the same time.

I said to him, "If you want this marriage to work, you have to be honest with me."

"I'm honest with you," he said.

"I know about your secret baby."

Hearing those words flow through my mouth caused me so much pain, I grew angry immediately.

He said, "I don't know anything about a baby, where are you getting this information from?"

"Your smartphone."

He yelled angrily, "I didn't come here for this. I just wanted to have a good time. You ruin everything, and I'm going home"!

At that moment, I knew I wasn't willing to compromise anymore. I also learned a valuable lesson: he would never be faithful, and it was enough for me just to let go and move forward. Sometimes the details can cause more pain. I knew the nature of his character and knew he wasn't ready to change.

Turning 40 was no longer about my children growing up or retiring. It was about me growing into a woman and living a life that is purpose-driven and not emotionally driven.

Just when I was turning 40, my trials and adversity gave me a new perspective about life. Sometimes we are given lemons in life, which can leave us bitter if we choose. However, I decided to make lemonade by adding some sweetener to my circumstances. I learned to forgive and live life in love no matter what life brings.

Now, this is 40!

HARRY, THE HORSE
Don Conway

Author's note: This is one of a series of stories called Movie Minor Characters in which I develop a fictional history of a minor character in a popular movie. Harry, the Horse, is such a person in the movie "Guys and Dolls."

Harry Goldfarb, later known as Harry the Horse, was raised in an Orthodox Jewish home in the Park Slope section of Brooklyn, New York. His father, Myron, was a staunch member of the local synagogue. His mother, Estelle, was a Hadassah member of long-standing. The family spoke, in order, Yiddish, English, and Russian at home. Harry was an only child, and, of course, his parents had great hopes and ambitions for their son. The problem was the Gowanus Canal. But more on that in a moment.

In 1912, the year Harry was born, there was a huge increase of Ashkenazi Jewish immigrants from Eastern and Central Europe to the United States, most of who settled in New York. Not all of the immigrants were of poor peasant stock. A small percentage of them were urban criminals from cities like Minsk, Bialystok, and Moscow. It was not unusual for some of these criminal types (sometimes referred to as the "Jewish Mafia") to anchor themselves in a local Jewish community. A few of them became members of the same synagogue as Myron and Estelle. The families often mingled at social events at the temple.

At age 13 Harry made his Bar Mitzvah along with his best friends Moe Edelmann and Izzy Goldstein, both sons of the temple's criminal element. Izzy's father was a guest of the State of New York at Sing Sing prison. Boys at age 13 have been known to defy their parents' commands. One of the strictest commands from the mothers of Park Slope boys was "Stay away from the Gowanus Canal, and, for God's sake, don't ever go swimming in it like those Irish Goyim kids do."

The Gowanus Canal evolved out the Gowanus Creek, a tidal inlet surrounded by marshes and meadows. As early as 1630, the Dutch government of New York allowed and encouraged commercial and industrial development alongside the creek. It was later deepened and widened to form the shipping canal. The canal is 1.8 miles long and runs through the Northwestern portion of the borough of Brooklyn. By 1920, it had become one of the most polluted bodies of water in the United States. Hence the mothers' warning to stay out of it.

But Brooklyn is Brooklyn. The summers are hot, and, Harry, Moe, and Izzy were teenagers. One August day, they decided to test the waters. Besides, it was necessary to show the Irish Goyim that Jews were just as tough as them. After a swim in the mega-polluted canal, the boys were beset with full-body rashes, breathing difficulties, sore throats and a mysterious white crust around their eyes.

Harry's father was furious. For the first time in his life,

he beat his son with a strap. That was the turning point in Harry's life. His reverence for his father turned to open rebellion. For the next four years, Harry and his father engaged in silent warfare. With Moe and Izzy as his allies, Harry turned to petty crime "just to show his father."

The Park Slope section of Brooklyn, with its easy access to the Brooklyn waterfront, was a hotbed of bootleg whiskey during Prohibition (1920 -1933). Harry, by then 19, became a truck driver for an Italian mobster. A police ambush netted Harry and a truckload of bootleg whiskey in 1931. His sentence was for 18 months in the new city prison on Riker's Island. Harry's father was in the courtroom the day Harry was sentenced. Upon hearing the guilty verdict and the prison sentence, Myron yelled out, "My son is dead. I have no son!" as Harry was led away.

Upon his release from prison in late 1933, Harry moved into a Manhattan apartment with his old friend Moe Edelman. Moe was convinced that playing the horses was the best, and easiest way to make money. All one needed, according to Moe, was one big break.

Their big break came, they thought, when they visited a horse auction just outside of Baltimore, Maryland. Based on an impulse they bid on, and won, a horse "that looked great." The horse was a year old gelding that they named Wonder Boy. They had Wonder Boy shipped to Belmont Park racetrack just outside of New York City.

But Harry and Moe's had a money problem. Training Wonder Boy to be a racehorse, along with boarding fees and veterinarian costs soon overwhelmed them. A trainer at the racetrack advised them to form a syndicate (meaning a partnership) of investors to raise money to cover Wonder Boy's expenses. Harry liked the idea, but Moe did not. Moe agreed to sell his half of Wonder Boy to Harry for a sum to be paid out of the horse's future winnings.

Harry, now the sole owner of Wonder Boy, set about finding investors for his syndicate. He began soliciting his pals up and down Broadway in Manhattan: Nicely-Nicely Johnson, Nathan Detroit (a big-time New York gambler), Little Augie, Feet Samuels, Dave the Dude, Miss Adelaide Stevenson and a few dolls from the Kit-Kat Club, and about 40 other Broadway regulars, all bought into the syndicate based on Harry's assurances of future winnings.

It never happened. Wonder Boy turned out to have a congenital lung problem and had to be put down about a year after Harry formed the syndicate. The Broadway regulars shrugged off the loss as part of the risk of the racehorse owner's life. As a sort of warning to future friends of Harry's, he was branded with the name Harry the Horse. The name stuck.

Down on his luck and with a devastating reputation, Harry the Horse was forced to take a job, for tips and gratuities, as a sort of host to visiting VIP of the criminal persuasion. Harry, the Horse, knew where all the dolls were and where all the action was along Broadway. Visiting VIPs were glad to have Harry the Horseshow them around New York.

It was in this line of work Harry the Horse found himself escorting Chicago mobster Big Jule to a crap game, organized by Nathan Detroit, at the New York Department of Sewer Works. At this game, Big Jule became entangled with Sky Masterson, another high-rolling New Yorker who was infatuated with Sergeant Sarah Brown of the Save a Soul Mission. All of which was skillfully depicted in the movie "Guys and Dolls."

FLYING BACKWARDS
Patti Thomas

In many ways, my sister and I are alike. And in many ways, we are different. There are eight years between us; thus, we grew up in different eras. Hers was the time of the shift dress and ankle-hugging pants. Mine was elephant-bell bottoms and smock tops. High school girls in my sister's day had short hair with perfect little curls on their cheeks. Girls during my high school days had long, straight, parted-down-the-middle-almost-in-the-eyes hair. We all wanted to look like Farrah Fawcett. None of us even came close. Many were the times my mom made me wear my sister's hand-me-downs. No big deal, right? Lots of little sisters get their big sisters' clothes. It was a bit mortifying, though, having to wear pedal pushers whilst all the other girls were wearing super cool bell bottoms. My mother was not moved by my mortification.

There are so many instances where my sister, Chris, "Chrissie" to me, and I have either said or done the exact same thing at the exact same time. It doesn't really even surprise us anymore. Perhaps the most startling example of this was when we were in a car together, and we both saw a jogger running through a park. At the same time we both said, "JoGARE." We were attempting to say "jogger" in French, which, by the way, neither of us spoke. But somehow we both simultaneously thought we'd try and in perfect unison declared, "Jo-

GARE." I'm writing this phonetically, hoping you'll get my drift. Upon further research, I've found that the actual translation of jogger into French is "joggeur." And I've listened to it, and it is NOT how we say it. (Frankly, I like the way we say it better than the real French way. My apologies, France.)

Having both studied music and chosen music-teaching careers, we also can make a song about anything. Anything. One summer we planned a surprise party for our brother's retirement and upcoming bicycling trip in Italy. We sang every planning detail to each other and systematically drove my husband crazy. To his chagrin, we did a lot of this singing and planning in his presence. He attested to the fact that he was relieved when the party was over, assuming the singing would cease. But inevitably we found some other mundane activity for which we could commence vocalizing. If we aren't singing, then we can be found tapping out rhythms on whatever surface is available. Kitchen counters, tables, car steering wheels, and thighs are just a few of the items we've converted into drum sets.

We were recently together in our hometown, celebrating our mom's 95th birthday. We ended our trip with a bit of shopping in Minneapolis at the Mall of America. My sister can out-shop your sister any day of the week! And I'm not too bad at it either.

If you've ever been to the Mall of America, you know that there is an amusement park in the middle. Chrissie has always been the more adventurous one. She loves to travel. I like to stay home. She wants to zip line across a jungle. I want to zip up my hoodie and sit on the couch. So you can probably guess who loves crazy amusement park rides and who doesn't. She was trying to get me to go on one ride with her, just one. I agreed. Just one.

I could see her looking with anticipation at a roller coaster that did a couple of loop-de-loops. No way. There was some other horror-machine that took you straight up vertically and then dropped you face down, also vertically. Not ever going to happen. We decided to walk through the park and check out all our options. Aha! I remembered a ride I could probably do! Swings!

I could handle swings! Chrissie said she'd even do something as boring as the Ferris Wheel with me, but thinking that might be too slow, we both agreed to go on the Backyardigan's Swing-Along. Goodnight. Two grown women were going on a kiddie ride. How embar-rassing. We did notice among the throngs of children; however, there was the occasional adult rider, so we knew it could be done. There was one odd thing about this ride though: Some of the swings faced backward. Who would want to swing backward? Not me. You can't see where you're going, for one thing. Part of the thrill of the ride (can a swing-along be "thrilling?") is the feel of flying through the air, up above all the other mere walk-ers on the ground. We got our tickets and got on the ride right away. We were at the tail end of a line, though, leaving us with last dibs on seats. Ideally, we'd find two together, facing forward. We'd be able to fly together and maybe even sing about it while we were up there! I nabbed a forward-facing swing, but the ones closest to it faced the opposite direction. It's not like we had all the time in the world to find the ideal set-up; I noticed another forward-facing swing a few swings ahead. I suggested my sister go grab that one. She declined and grabbed a backward-facing one. "I'd rather be next to you," she said.

We took our seats, strapped ourselves in and pre-pared for the Backyardigans ride of our lives. We went up nice and high; it was pretty cool up there, flying. I know I had a big grin on my face. If I could choose a superpower for myself, I'd choose the ability to fly. Since I'm not counting on that actually happening, the swing-along might be as close as I come.

As we were finishing the ride, it occurred to me that my sister had forfeited not only a thrilling ride but had even given up any chance of it even being fun so she could sit next to me.

Sometimes "I love you" can come in unexpected and ordinary ways, liking choosing to fly backward so you can be by your sister.

If anyone should have gone backward, it was I. She was the one wanting the amusement ride in the first place. But she gave up her thrill of going upside down on a roller coaster and then even gave up the action of facing forward on the swings. It might not say, "I love you" to everyone, but it did to me.

In many ways, my sister and I are alike. And in many

ways, we are different.

Chrissie, I always want to sit next to you, too.

CONFESSION OF AN AGE JUNKIE

Shelley Leiman

I'm from Brooklyn. If youse guys don't know about Brooklyn, I'll tell you somethin. It ain't like no uddah place. Ya gotta be careful whatcha say. And when ya meet a new guy, ya don't ask no questions. He could have what youse guys call "connections."

So there's this guy I met at a choich dance, and we "hit it off." I liked him, and he said he liked me a lot. So we saw each uddah a few times. We didn't know nothin poysonal about each uddah. Den one night he asked me how old I was. I was shocked! Hey, what kinda guy has the noyve to ask a middle-aged lady a ting like that! I made out I didn't hear him. Again he said, "Hey, Sis, how old are ya?" Well, lots of times when someone asked me dat poisonal question, I'd tell him "I'd rather not say" or "It is just a numbah." So I quietly lied to my new friend. You might say I weaved my tangled web if ya know what I mean. For years, I was told I looked and behaved much youngah than my crony logic age and always lived by my biologic age. Sometimes I'd say I'm toydy nine. [If it was good enough for Jack Benny, it was good enough for me.]

But I felt a terrible pain in my gut after I lied to him, and den it was too late! It was as if some evil spirit invaded me and needed to be exorcised! I guess ya know what that means! But how? Who could help me!

"But wait a minute", I thought, "Maybe I could do it myself. I could exorcise this evil spirit by telling him the trute. And ya know what? Dis could be da first self-exorcism in choich history." Right? So I wrote him dis note:

"I don't know how ya will react to this confession, so maybe multiple chers would be in order. Take your pick!

1. Age. Schmage, who cares!
2. So just how many years did you shave off?
3. This is unforgivable!
4. If I had known…
5. None of the above
6. All of the above

He knocked at the door, I handed him the note, and what do you tink he did?

He touched his finga to his forehead, shook his head from side to side, and said, "Let's go! I'm hungry!

THE TEA CUP

Betty Jean Kult

She stubs her toe and falls, her hand-me-down shoes too big for her feet, but they are from her cousin, so she's wearing them. Sophie's mum had said, "You will grow into them soon enough." She had scraped her knees, and the blood is trickling down her leg. It hurts, and she wants to cry, but she has to be brave and finish the task her mother has given her to do.

She looks around for a minute and spots something out of place. It was a box under a bush. Maybe something was in it her mum could use. She slowly gets up and goes to the bush.

Sophie is only eight years old, tiny and thin, and lives in London. It is the late 1700's.

Today she has been walking the neighborhood looking for pieces of coal for her mum. Sometimes the coal trucks are so overloaded they drop pieces along the roadside.

Sophie picks up the box and, thinking she has found something special, puts it in her coal bucket.

As she goes on her way, Sophie looks down at her package and notices a label with a name and address on it.

The words of her mum come to her mind—if it isn't a gift and you know whom it belongs to, it isn't yours. After thinking this over for a while, Sophie decides she must return the package to its rightful owner. The address is not too far from where she is, and she sets off on foot. Reaching the address Sophie is in awe of the lovely home. The beautiful decorative wooden door has a large metal knocker. It is too high for little Sophie to reach so she knocks as hard as she can. Luckily someone inside hears the knock.

A friendly looking middle-aged woman opens the door, and a look of surprise crosses her face. What she sees is a little raggedy street urchin with scraped knees and a smudged dirty face and hands. Immediately she feels concern and compassion for this little child. The woman finds her voice and says, "Oh my, how did you hurt yourself, child?"

"I fell but, I found your package," Sophie says.

"Me package, where?" says the woman.

"Aside from the road."

The woman pauses and contemplates what Sophie has said. "That is so thoughtful of you to bring it to me," the woman says. "Would you like to come in?"

The woman seems kind and concerned, but Sophie's mum had warned her not to take up with strangers.

"I can't," says Sophie, "But, thank you, ma'am."

The woman smiles sweetly, and Sophie thinks she understands.

"Well, why don't we just sit here on the porch a bit and I will open the package."

Sophie is quite curious, and she sits down. The woman pauses and says, "Before I open it I have to do something, but I'll be right back," as she turns and goes back inside the house.

She returns carrying a small basin of water, some salve, and bandages. She sits down next to Sophie and begins attending to her wounds. It stings, but Sophie knows the woman is helping her. As the woman bandages her knees, she talks to Sophie.

"Now, young lady, what might your name be?

"Me name is Sophie,"

"Me name is Sybil. Tis nice to meet ya."

"Thank you, ma'am."

"Now why is this coal so important to ya, Sophie?"

"Me mum needs it to heat our home and cook our food."

"Oh, I see," says Sybil. "Well, why don't we open this here package now?" Sybil takes a knife and slits open the box.

She reaches inside the box and takes out something wrapped in layers of tissue paper. Unpeeling the layers, she holds up a very lovely, delicate purple-flowered teacup.

Sophie's mouth opens wide as she let out a gasp, "Tis beautiful. I've never seen a teacup like that before."

"Doesn't your mum drink tea, Sophie?"

"Oh that she does, ma'am, but, her cup is metal, it has no handle, and it almost always burns her fingers!"

"Oh my, poor thing!" says Sybil.

They sat quiet for a bit, and then Sophie stands up and says, "I had better go, me mum will be looking fur me."

"Yes, we dun't want to worry her but, I 'ave enjoyed meeting ya, Sophie."

"Me too ma'am and thank ya for fixing me knees."

Sybil wraps up the cup and returns it to the box and puts it in Sophie's coal pail. Sophie looks at Sybil with surprise in her eyes. "Oh no mam, I can't take your cup"

"Yes, I want you to 'ave it, you 'ave been so sweet to bring it to me even though you were hurt. "You may keep it or give it to your mum so she won't burn her fingers."

Tears came to Sophie's eyes as the woman reaches to hug her. "Thank ya so much, ma'am."

Sophie hurries home as if she's walking on a cloud.

It just so happens that Sophie's mother is having a birthday. Sophie has been sad because she hasn't been planning to give her mum something. But now she has a present for her, a very special present indeed!

INHERITANCE
Ginny Smythe

Your departure left me unmoored
The wind died, and my sail emptied
I had to swim and tug the boat to shore
Lungs to capacity with ferocious tenacity
But still floundering under the heavy weight

I was left rudderless for a few seasons
The one to yell 'coming about' was gone
You had always been my captain and my anchor
But you also left destruction and self-doubt in your wake
It took perseverance and the passage of time to find the way

Chasing your approval ever since I can remember
For years, I felt unworthy, less than, not enough
I tacked back and forth seeking validation and recognition
Why couldn't you have been proud?
Never holding back disapproval, you were always loud.

The confidence you left in your wake was swallowed up by
the sea
Couldn't you have left a few crumbs for me?
Perhaps, your unmet expectations are my inheritance.
But could your confidence have all been a con?
I cannot know the truth now that you are gone.

My distorted view has wreaked havoc on my life
Your teasing and bullying ways always cut like a knife
Historical truth is no longer my mission
I am learning—it is an unwarranted condition
The next buoy is in sight, so I will continue to share my
light.

I no longer need to weather this inheritance.

SUGAR
Hartley Barnes

Dear Sugar,

    If my honesty seems brutal, please forgive me. I am dead. It will be said I died for my country and I am a hero, as they say about all men who die in service of their homeland. I am not a hero; I am a man who did the right thing to take care of his daughter. The country is secondary. The sacrifice I made was not patriotism for my nation. It was for you. I choose to serve my country to provide for you to ensure your future.

    In the basement of my head, tucked away in a cell, is the day of your conception. You were not part of the plan; it was more about lust. I am glad you came; you gave me a chance to love someone special. I did not die in vain. I died so you can live. My death is not deliberate; it's one of the risks taken when Daddies go to war. For the short time, we have been together I cherish every second. I carried with me your first cry, your Mona Lisa smile, first steps, the first day of school, and all your hugs.

    We have a library of memories exclusive only to us; draw on them for strength when days are not good. Tickle yourself with the funny ones, and if you need to cry, do it knowing I am next to you with your hand in mine. Do not dwell on my passing; use it as an encouragement to build a better you.

I am one block of your foundation. It is a start. Create and construct, look back only for inspiration and nothing else. Reflect on the positives and use them for walking on. Be kind, gracious, and spread yourself like the sun. Warm the hearts of those around you. If you are asked about me, smile, and if tears fall, it's okay. Say I am standing next to you—I am.

Should you have children do not say to them I am a hero. Tell them about our time together. Tell them I loved you, and I would have loved them as much as you do.

We will meet in the future.

NO SIREN? NO LIGHTS?
John F. Rifenberg

They shut the door of the ambulance with me in it. I'm not feeling that great. For some reason, I notice the ceiling of the vehicle. It's just like the movies; the camera pans over the patient with the medics busy doing whatever they're supposed to be doing. Then the camera moves to the silver metal ceiling harboring bright, round lights and the siren starts to wail. The lights dim as they charge away to save the poor guy.

Backing out of my driveway, they seem to be in no hurry. Why isn't the siren blaring or lights flashing? I live two doors from a stop sign. They'll probably just run the stop sign and head directly to the hospital. They know the fastest route. Everyone knows to go to Crestwood Street and go south- it's the fastest route.

They stop at the stop sign. What! Let's pretend that this is an ambulance! I hope the driver isn't lost.

A voice breaks the spell.

"What's your name?"

"John Francis Rifenberg."

"Where do you live?"

"We just left my house. You know where I live. Who's driving? Where are the siren and lights?"

I'm hoping this isn't a heart attack, but I know it's better than having a stroke. A stroke is like a curse from an ex-wife. You are wounded badly, but you live. The medics keep asking me questions.

"Are you in pain?"

"No, nauseous and dizzy as hell…but no pain."

Now, comes the classic line that everyone loves to hear at this time in his or her life. "If you had to measure your pain, with ten being the worst, what number would you say?"

I had to laugh even though it hurt. "I'm divorced; I had my wallet ripped from my body, right through my beaten and battered my heart by my ex-wife's lawyers. Compared to that, this is about a two."

One of the medics was in the background calling the hospital to give someone my situation. It's a bunch of numbers. I didn't know if they were good or bad. Then I thought …why aren't they driving faster? Still neither lights nor siren. Oh crap! Maybe I died, and I don't know it. It's an out-of-body experience; this is how it must feel. Another voice chimes in denying my death.

"How old are you?"

"I'm going to be 72 this year."

"Have you used Viagra or something similar in the last 24 to 36 hours?"

"I wish!"

This one voice seemed to be the one in charge of this journey. I motioned the voice over to me.

"How fast is this guy driving? What route is he using? The hospital isn't that far. Am I having a stroke?"

The voice says confidently, "We are almost there; the traffic is heavy at this hour."

I'm thinking, wait a minute, this is an ambulance; we can drive as fast as we want. The only thing that's better than an ambulance is a black and white police car with, dare I say it …the siren blasting and, God for, bid all the lights on, complete with bright shining colors.

"Mr. Rifenberg, you are fine. Your blood pressure is going a little crazy. We now have it under control, but, we have to check you out because of your age."

My age? If I hear that one more time, I'm going to kill myself. Then I have a really terrible thought. I ask, "Do I have to pay for this ride. All of a sudden, I'm feeling sick again.

The voice then announces,

"His blood pressure is going crazy again."

"The voice then says to me "Not really, your health insurance will handle most of the cost. Stop talking and relax. We are almost there. I'm sure you can pay for it. You have a beautiful home."

"That's my wife's house, and she's the artist. Damn! I wish I had half of her money."

"Yes, that just means that you are happily married like the rest of us."

I knew right away that I liked this voice. Maybe I made a friend.

"Just a thought, because I don't hear a siren and this guy driving isn't in a hurry. I'm just trying to get my money's worth if you know what I mean."

Once more the voice states,

"OK, we're here. That wasn't too bad."

"Yes, this just makes my day. Was that thunder I just heard?"

"It's starting to rain."

"I can't get a break…there's a downpour outside. If the incompetent driver had put on the lights or the damn siren, we would have beaten the storm. Please, tell me you have an umbrella. I don't want to get wet in my condition.

"I think I know why you have blood pressure problems. Calm down! Everything is going to be alright. We're under the emergency room canopy."

"Are you sure? Great! When they're done with me, let's go have a beer."

The voice answers, "I think we have had enough quality time together. And I don't know the fastest route to the local tavern, and there will be no sirens and no lights."

THE DANCE I DANCED

Karina G. Felix

It was coming
I could feel it
The dance I'll dance
To clear it all away

It's time
Makeup on
Hair done
Little black dress fits
Red four-inch pumps

I sashay into the room
They stare in awe
I move slowly to the center
He grabs me tight

We waltz, foxtrot,
Two-step and salsa.
We glide and float
Throughout the room

The music builds
We see just us
Spinning, whirling,
Twirling and dipping

I'm dancing the dance
That lets me let go
The issues of the world
No more

The music slows
We come back to earth
Our feet touch the ground
As he fades into the sound

I run here
I run there
But he's gone

And with him
The music but not
The memory of
The dance I danced

ISN'T SHE LOVELY?
Virginia Guido

Jessica impatiently tapped her fingers on the leather chair. She looked around the room, rolled her eyes, and sighed.

"Jessica!" Dr. Ortega tried to get her attention. "You always seem so uncooperative and negative during your visits here. I'm sure you must have one cheerful thought or recollection on which you might focus. Do you have a happy childhood memory that you could share with me?"

She screwed up her face in deep thought., snapped her fingers, and said, "Okay, I got one!"

"Tell me about it. Please."

"It isn't just a happy childhood memory. It's one of my greatest childhood memories. Still, it was bittersweet. I learned a valuable lesson from it, too.

"Right after I turned four, my dad came home on leave. During this time, he was bored because Mom was at work, my sisters were in school, and Grandma didn't speak English, so with nothing to do, he starts teaching me how to read and write." She leaned in closer to Dr. Ortega. "And I mean cursive writing, not printing. He showed me how to add and subtract numbers. My dad even bought a chalkboard so I could have the complete classroom experience."

"And that was your great childhood memory?"

"No! That was just the appetizer. It was the attention that I loved. The more I learned, the happier my dad was. He was so proud of me. So he asked me what I would like to do as a reward for being such a good student."

"What did you ask for?"

"I asked for an experience. I really wanted to see the movie "Sleeping Beauty." It was playing at a theater downtown. Mom never took us to frivolous shows, especially downtown. She said local movies are cheaper and they give away free sets of dishes.

"I also asked him if I could have a white dress, black patent leather t-strap shoes, and those little socks edged with lace. I wanted something that wasn't a hand-me-down."

"Did you get everything you requested?"

Jessica's eyes shone as she spoke. "Oh, yes! Daddy bought me a pretty white dress, the perfect shoes, and lacy socks. He took me downtown by bus. During our ride, he asked me to read all the ads above the windows. After I finished, he turned to the passengers and told them, 'She just turned four.' Everyone murmured approval. Some even clapped. I was "Daddy's Girl" for the day, his little princess, an only child out on the town in her brand new clothes. It was the greatest day of my pathetic little life."

"You said you learned a lesson that day. Do you recall the lesson?"

Jessica frowned and spoke slowly. There was a sadness laced with anger in her voice. "When we got home, Mom was there. She took one look at me and my new outfit and got so mad. At that moment, my mom looked like Maleficent, the evil queen from "Sleeping Beauty." She started shouting, 'Fred, what is the baby wearing? Where did she get those clothes? Better yet, where did you get the money for this? You didn't squander my rent money on that foolish purchase, did you? Who buys a toddler a white dress? That child cannot stay clean for thirty seconds. What were you thinking? Why would you do such a stupid thing? Answer me, Fred!'"

She put her head down. "I watched my dad deflate a little with each question. I waited for him to tell her it was my reward because of how well I could read. He need-ed to say how smart I was. I screamed inside, 'Daddy, please, give me a number problem, show her what I can do!'"

Looking up, Jessica said, "But he didn't stand up to her. He practically shrank in her presence. He told her, 'You're right, Ro. I should have asked your permission before I indulged my daughter. I'm sorry. It won't happen ever again.' That's what he said, and it was true because my dad shipped out the next day and disappeared from our lives. Permanently."

Dr. Ortega waited for her to finish.

"I never wore that outfit again. I think my mom tried to return it. But she couldn't eradicate the lesson those clothes taught me. I learned you couldn't rely on others to defend you or stand up for you. That's why I'm inclined to speak up for myself and for things I believe. I don't wait for someone else to speak in my defense. That may not ever happen. I really don't trust many people or accept what they say as truth. Now you know why my skeptical attitude leaves a lot to be desired. Especially when I'm told 'This won't hurt a bit.'"

"Did you ever discuss this with anyone in your family?"

"Nope, and I never will. This is the first and only time that I've told that story. "

"Well, thank you for opening up to me. You just have to work harder on getting along with others. Be part of a team."

"I'll try, Doctor. Seriously, I will. I'm glad we sat down and cleared the air. Please apologize to your assistant for me when you visit her at the hospital. It was not my intention to bite her, but she did remind me of my mother. Now, I believe all this started when I requested a double dose of Novocain for my molar extraction. Do I get it now or must I get hostile again?"

HEART BEAT
Tajuana Troy

My heart beats for love and integrity
I am emotionally relaxed
Anxiousness did flee
Restlessness will never be

I'm grateful for all I see
I smile at the sunset
Nature gives me pleasure
I enjoy pareidolia in the sky

The sound of the sea relaxes me
Jazz is soothing to my soul
I write for meditation
The lyrics are freedom in sync with my heartbeat

MINNIE BOTTOMS

Shelley Leiman

"Did you hear about Minnie Bottoms?"

"No, what?"

"She's been arrested for bank theft!"

"Not our gal, Minnie?!"

A small group of townspeople began to assemble outside of the sheriff's office, visibly shocked by the news. A few others tended to believe it and didn't mind expressing their opinions.

"Remember that time a young fella came to town and Minnie seemed to change?"

"Yes, she stopped wearing those orthopedic shoes and got real cool eyeglasses!"

"And she ate lunch at the local Duffy's nearly every day."

"It must have cost her a pretty penny. She used to brown-bag lunch."

"And where did she get the money to contribute $1,000 to the Christmas Wish Fund?"

Most people who knew the real Minnie did not share these suspicions. She was born in Centerville 60 years ago and led a modest life, exemplifying the town's con-servatism. Although socially shy, she was nevertheless a "people person." As a teller at the bank since high school graduation, she was acquainted with most of the residents; as a friend, she often became involved in their lives when they asked for her help. When she won at bingo, her enthusiasm was limitless. She loved movies, but not the smell of popcorn and rancid butter. Playing bridge once a week with seven other people was probably the highlight of her social life. Although she was not a good player, she enjoyed the mental challenges it provided and looked forward to spending an evening with friends. Everyone tolerated her errors because they cared for her. She always tried to facilitate good-will among them that, if you know bridge, is a necessary component. Her little Cape Cod home, where she spent most of her leisure time with her two cats, was her private world. There she enjoyed many sewing projects. Store-bought clothes were not for her, as witnessed by the eight identical dresses she had made for herself, each in a different color but from the same pattern.

Although she loved to read, she was limited by poor eyesight. Longing to be in a loving relationship, it had eluded her. This was the Minnie Bottoms most people knew. She was always on time, rain or shine, walked briskly down the street to the bank each day, proudly carried her lunch bag with her peanut butter and jelly sandwich, greeted everyone she passed, waved to the children at the school bus stop and regularly chastised the little boys; she could sniff out teasing before it happened. Her tone of voice was clear and gentle, ideal for reading bible stories to eager children on Sunday afternoons. Once inside the bank, she prepared her station and performed her duties professionally, pleasantly, and efficiently.

But this day was different. Someone had seen the sheriff escorting her out of the bank to his office down the street. Speculation was rampant, and a noisy crowd gathered outside the sheriff's office. The time seemed endless, but soon the sheriff left his office with Minnie and lawyer John Blake. The group walked back to the bank and went into a meeting room where bank officials had gathered. Uncontrollable tears ran down Minnie's cheeks. Her nose was red from the harshness of her handkerchief. Someone offered her water, but she refused with a wave of her hand. She patted her skirt and then her shirt pocket, trying to locate her eyeglasses that were on top of her head. An unnatural quiet filled the room.

Using real money, she was asked to demonstrate how she handles a typical bank deposit, a withdrawal, and reconciliation at the end of a day. The group stood in silence, paying close attention. But then there were barely audible sounds of disbelief! It became obvious that Minnie mistook $20 bills for tens! Her poor vision had created havoc! There was a cacophony of angry voices. The bank officials huddled together, hoping for a team decision. After several minutes, she was informed that she could no longer be trusted as a teller and was urged to resign rather than be fired. Her voice choked as she tried to apologize.

"Oh no, please don't fire me," she pleaded. An unnatural quiet filled the room. After a lengthy discussion, it was agreed to place Minnie in another department where she would greet and assist customers but would not be involved in money transactions. You see, there wasn't a soul in Centerville who would have dreamed of hurting their Minnie. In a town of 20,000 residents, it could honestly be said that in her lifetime, she had endeared herself to at least one-quarter of the population in a personal way.

YOU LEFT US TOO SOON

Ginny Smythe

You left us too soon.
We didn't get a goodbye.
You left us too soon.
You made everyone cry.

And now:
The room is a little bit quieter
There is less laughter, less light

There are fresh tears and heavy hearts in this familiar
space
There is the tradition of raising glasses to celebrate a life

Reminiscing about days when we were all together.
Storytelling of cotillions, professors, campus, and cock-
tails
Recognizing you always made time for each of us with
your open door

And now:
The stories morph — grandchildren, jobs, new aches,
and pains.
Hugging old friends tight with promises to visit and
write.

You left us too soon.

You didn't get to see.
The integration of the groups—the A and the B

We've found a common thread through you, our college
friend

You saw people's souls, not status or clout
You loved us wholly and without any doubt

So kind of heart, so generous of soul
What do we do now? Where do we go?
So quick to forgive and so full of strength
Many would have folded or run for the hills
You stood strong through your storm and never looked ill.

I will always remember your no judgement zone
when we laughed and cried for hours over the phone.

A volunteer, a mother, and a friend
Such promise, such brilliance, such a premature end

No service, no flowers just as you wished
We will hug your children for you
As we bid you adieu

You left us too soon with so much left to do.
We all still want to know what you knew.

You left ME too soon.
And now, I'll think of you when I look at the moon.

THE TRUMPET BLOWS

Hartley Barnes

They lined up behind the Trumpet, giving it their approval and exposing their bigotry. The Trumpet blows at the woman and their private parts, at the mothers of our fallen soldiers with disrespect. Immigrants disparaged and children separated from families. Athletes ridiculed for standing up for their right to protest.

Disabled mocked for pointing to the truth, and a black woman is called a dog. It takes one to know one. The media characterized as fake and the followers gloat with mocking laughter. Opponents invited to a hero's funeral and the Trumpet consigned to irrelevancy and shunned. There is much more to come.

Hate groups are empowered to spread their wings and feel comfortable spewing venomous words in public. Trumpism is a microcosm of the part of our land that still believes in white supremacy. Our country is divided by a Trumpet out of tune and laughed at around the globe. The ignoramus Trumpet continues to pout and show its colors.

America is now the headless stallion, willing to cave in to its adversaries for the sake of the Trumpet's ego. The Trumpet refuses to call out the Kremlin for interfering in American politics. Why condemn the Russians, they are helping this instrument take center stage and make a mockery of American democracy? What do they

have on the tarnished Trumpet? Each note played is pre-
ceded by polluted air and third-grade rhetoric. Ice cream
words from a pompous president have no basis or value.
It has nothing but emptiness.

The spineless Republicans hypnotized by fear cannot
think for themselves; except one or two, they refuse to
stand up. Partisan politics is the catch of the day with
the hook baited with intimidation. The example set by
the Trumpet will take hold of the unsuspecting, to be
accepted and practiced in the future, broadening narcissistic ideology. The tornado on Pennsylvania Avenue is
self-serving and comfy with Moscow. America is in dan-
ger.

The Trumpet is nothing more than restitution by racist
America for putting a black man in the Oval Office. Look
at what is in there now— a wannabe dictator, a buffoon
who along with his despicable base bamboozled the
weak ones in our nation to elect a rusted Trumpet.

The Trumpet blows.

IT'S ONLY A PIECE OF METAL
John F. Rifenberg

Automobiles, everyone has memories
Your very first car, in your name!
Those old cars that seemed to run forever
At least in our minds
My 1968 Chevy Bel Air, with four doors and AM radio
Its color was a worn-out shade of blue
I went everywhere in that car.
Powered by a 283-V8 motor, that started every time
Every day was a new experience
Sex education class was held in the back seat
Buying vinyl records
New and exciting color TV
A man walked on the Moon.

I remember that day, it was sad
She had cancer in her motor
A man with a smelly cigar and wearing a dirty shirt told
me
"She's all used up.
But, I took real good care of her.
Sorry, she's pretty old, lots of miles."
I took a real long look at her; she did look tired and worn
Wiping his dirty hands with a dirty rag
He looked at me, looking at her
"It's only a piece of metal."

It was obvious to me the man knew nothing about automobiles.

I'D RATHER DIE
Karina G. Felix

That's it! I've had it!
I'd rather die.

I could take the emotional abuse
I could take the mental abuse.
I could even take the physical abuse
But I was not going to live in fear anymore.
I'd rather die.

I was not going to let fear freeze me in place.
I was not going to let fear paralyze me again.
I was not going to let fear cover the unseen bruises.
I was not going to let fear design my life.
I'd rather die.

I gave up control.
I gave up hiding.
I gave up fear…
And struck back.

In return
I paralyzed him.
I transferred that fear
And regained my life.

ECONOMICS 101- BROOKLYN STYLE
Don Conway

Imagine you are a vintner in Sicily. You produce an okay wine labeled Chianti Straccali. It costs you $4.50 per bottle to produce. Because there is so much local competition, it sells for $6.00 a bottle anywhere in Italy. At Olive Garden restaurants in the United States it sells for $23 a bottle. So, of course, you decide to ship 500 cases (3,000 bottles) to New York. Your shipping costs, including insurance, are $2.50 per bottle. Your investment for production and shipping is $7.00 per bottle or $21,000 for the 3,000 bottles.

When the ship carrying your wine arrives at the dock in Brooklyn, longshoremen unload it. To work on the Brooklyn docks, you must belong to the Longshoremen's Union, which is controlled by the Martorano mafia family. (How the Martorano's got control of the union is another story). Union dues are $500 per month. You must also pay a kickback to the union shop steward for each day you work.

The shop steward system: The number of ships going in and out of port varies from day to day, which means the number of workers needed to unload and load the ships varies as well. To accommodate this variation, there is a "Morning Shape-up" every day at 7:00 am. All long-shoremen willing to work gather at a meeting place and the shop steward selects the men to work that day...

hence the kickback to the shop steward if you want to work. Non-union workers get work only in an extreme emergency, such as a banana boat with ripening fruit that must be unloaded ASAP.

So the ship carrying your wine has docked, and the workers have been chosen to unload your 3,000 bottles of Chianti Straccali. For fragile items, like wine bottles, it is assumed there will be some breakage due to the rigors of loading, unloading, and a hazardous sea voyage. Through some tense negotiations between the insurance agent and two very large gentlemen from the Martorano family, it has been agreed that, for your shipment, 50 cases (300 bottles), will have been "broken." The insurance company is happy to reimburse you $1,500 for these "broken" bottles. While this reduces the insurance company's profit they are aware that all 3,000 bottles could have been broken.

As predicted, 25 cases (300 bottles) of your wine were broken while being unloaded from the ship. For safekeeping, the 300 bottles were moved to the back room of the union/mafia/ office. A New York wine merchant purchased the remaining 2,700 unbroken bottles for $15 per bottle ($40,500). The Olive Garden restaurant in Brooklyn (franchise owned by cousin Vito) bought 150 bottles from the mafia for $20 per bottle ($3,000) and subsequently sold them for $23. The remaining 150 "broken" bottles were sold to three Italian restaurants in Brooklyn (who happened to be enjoying mafia "protection") for $23 per bottle (subsequently sold for $30). As a good-will gesture, and a promise of future business, the mafia paid you $1,500 for the 300 bottles ($5 per bottle).

PROFIT AND LOSS STATEMENT

Vintner (3,000 bottles)

<u>Expense</u>
<u>Income</u>
3000 bottles x $4.50 ea   = $13,500
Shipping 3000 bottles x $2.50 =   7,500
               Total expense $21,000

Reimbursement from Insurance Co. 300 bottles @ $5.00ea = $1,500

Sales to NY wine merchant 2700 bottles @ $15.00ea += $40,500
Reimbursement from Mafia 300 bottles @ $5.00ea = $1500
Total income $43,500

Profit = Income less expense ($43,500 - $21,000) = $22,500

Mafia (300 bottles)
Expense
Income
               $ 0.00

150 bottles to Brooklyn Olive Garden @ $20.00ea =
$3,000

50 bottles to "protected" restaurants @ $23ea = $3,450

Total income $ 6,450

Profit = income less expense ($6450 - $0.00) = $6,450

NY wine merchant

Expense

Income

2700 bottles @ $15.00 = $40,500

2700 bottles @ $19.00 = $ 51,300

Profit = ($51, 300 – $40.500) = $10,800

Olive Garden Brooklyn

Expense

Income

150 bottles @ $20.00ea = $3,000

150 bottles @ $23,00ea = $3,450

Profit = ($3,400 - $3,000) = $450.00

Economic Lessons Learned

Close examination of the profit and loss statement leads
to the following conclusions:

    A. By including the mafia in these business transac-
tions, significant social and economic benefits accrue
to the longshoremen working on the Brooklyn docks
and their families. It is noted that these benefits
occur with a minimum expenditure of resources and/

or capital.

B. Sicilian vintners stand to gain significant profits by selling in the United States rather than in local outlets. These profits, in turn, allow the vintners to reinvest in their undertakings with consequent social and economic benefits all the way up their distribution chain.

C. While profits will be diminished for insurance companies, it is widely accepted that their loss is society's gain.

JUST A SMILE
Betty Jean Kult

A smile doesn't take a lot of effort, but it means so much,
It's almost like getting a tender touch
Remember the last time someone smiled your way
I bet it made a difference in your day.
Remember the person's face seemed bright and cheery
Their continence was not at all dreary
So come on, give up and show your dimple or
Maybe your face is just plain and simple
Just enjoy that good feeling they have unlocked
It doesn't matter if you are young or old
You will feel better when your face you unfold.
The next time you feel your face start to frown
You will see it smile when you turn it upside down.
We are all in this same ole boat
So try and smile and get some hope,
And don't let the world get your goat!

PINK LEMONADE
Virginia Guido

When you're an adult, a lot of research is involved in finding your favorite drink. There are numerous taste tests to be conducted. You may find yourself crawling on the floor looking for your information-laden clipboard before realizing you had no such clipboard!

My favorite potent potable is known as "The Sicilian Kiss," which is comprised of three parts Amaretto and two parts Southern Comfort. The smooth, but lethal blend is an homage to my Italian mother and South-ern-born father. Although this is my preferred alcoholic drink, it is not my most unforgettable beverage.

The most memorable thirst-quencher is my mom's "Coney Island Pink Lemonade." Every weekend in the summer; my mother would practically drag my sisters and me to Coney Island Beach. The ritual before this excursion was to pack the prepared sandwiches and then mix the pink lemonade in the red bubble-shaped thermos jug. Mom was meticulous about the pre-beach protocol and would supervise our every move.

"Clean plastic cups?'

"Check."

"Towels and beach toys?"

"Check."

"All sandwiches and napkins in the beach tote?"

"Yeah."

"Say 'Yes, please.'"

"Does the jug have enough ice?"

"Yes, please." (Yeah, we were smart alecks)

"Okay, let's go!"

After two buses and one train ride, we arrived at the seashore "dying of thirst." We unwrapped the clear, clean, plastic cups and poured the sweet lemony nectar into them. Aah! We savored the coolness of the liquid, felt the pulp of the lemons drifting around our tongue, and relished the tartness and then CRUNCH. We tasted the sand.

"Mom, there's sand in my drink."

"You probably got some in the cup."

"No, the cups are clean. We just unwrapped them."

"Well, then whoever was the last one to wash the jug didn't do such a good job, did she?"

"Um, that would be you, Mom."

"Oh, maybe Minute Maid has added granulated sugar to its frozen concentrate."

"No, Mom, this is definitely sand."

"Let me see that jug."

We handed over the red bubble thermos to mom and watched as she inspected the inside, looking for the tiniest trace of sand. There was none to be found. She checked each cup and discovered each one lacking in grainy particles. Then she poured a cup of pink lemonade and held it up to the sunlight. We all stared at the cup along with a few of the sunbathers on nearby blankets.

The lemonade radiated a pink glow as small bits of pulp wafted like juicy snowflakes through the rosy mixture. Still, there was no trace of sand in that cup. Mom took a sip and swirled it around her mouth. We could almost taste the cool, sugary drink with her. She slowly swished the liquid from cheek to cheek and frowned.

Mom swallowed the beverage and made a face. "Well, what do you know? There's sand in this drink. I'll be damned if I know how it got there."

Every summer after that, for the rest of my childhood, my sisters and I acclimated our taste buds to accept the chilled pink lemonade with a crunch. No matter how we cleaned that jug, the sand always found its way into our drink.

The mystery was never solved, and the thermos is long gone, but my memory still readies me for that crunch every time I drink pink lemonade. I'm disappointed just to taste lemonade.

After all, like mom used to joke, "What's a cool drink on the beach without the sand, which is (sandwiches) there?"

SCRIBBLES

Tajuana Troy

I'm not a rapper
Nor a poet
I just have a memoir
I don't want to be labeled

I don't want parameters on what I write
I directly capture the organic moments of my life
I like to be expressive in my thoughts
It's healing for me

I have an outlet to be authentic
I can revisit my space without judgment
I can reflect on growth from moment to moment
I can capture my thoughts with words

I write exactly what I feel
My words are testimonies of my experiences
The beauty of it all
They are scribbles to others but life-changing moments
for me

DADDY

Shelley Leiman

A five-year-old girl was getting sleepy, waiting for her father to come home from work. She longed to be lifted up high for that special kiss and hug. But something was different that night and for many subsequent nights.

"Where is Daddy? When is he coming home?" she asked. "Tomorrow is Halloween, and I want to show him my princess costume."

Her big sister said their father had to work far away for a while, but he would come home soon. Then came Thanksgiving and Christmas and birthdays, all without him. It was painful for her to see her friends with their fathers, but she tried not to cry. She closed her eyes and imagined he was holding her in his arms as she traced his mustache with her little fingers and smelled his cheek as he held her close.

One day as she was bringing the newspaper in from the porch, she saw a picture on the front page. She could not read yet, but she was sure she knew who this was.

"Oh Daddy, it's you!" she gasped, and put her lips on his and kissed him, over and over again. She stood there for several minutes, thinking what to do. This would be her secret. She tore the picture from the paper as carefully as a young child could, and took it to her bedroom.

There, she gently placed it in her special drawer where she kept all her treasures. For many years it became her daily ritual to take it out, kiss it and talk to her Daddy.

As she grew into womanhood, the picture became a vague memory, lost amidst the complexities of life. Then one day, she found it among her forgotten treasures. As she held it in her trembling hands, she could not subdue a gentle smile. Holding it closer, she read a name beneath the image, the name she could not read as a young child. She gasped in disbelief! It took her several minutes to realize what had happened so many years ago. Her eyes began to tear… she felt short of breath… she leaned against the bureau for support and focused on the face. She tried to accept the truth. Again she read the name. This was not her Daddy! It was Charles de Gaulle! This picture she had found so many years ago had saved her from a childhood of pain and grief.

But now the time had finally come to mourn. And so she wept.

A JOYFUL NOISE
Gloria H. Ferrara

The house is quiet; the stair rail shinny slick as glass. All is perfect, just as she wanted; neat, tidy, calm.

Climbing the long stairway, she holds on to the rail with one hand as she leans on her cane steadying herself with the other. One, two three she counts until she reaches the landing in twelve steps. Pausing to catch her breath, she looks around the vast second landing where four bedrooms wait in silence.

This was a home once. Now it's just a house, a place she roams day and night from the lower level to the second landing. Clean beds covered with sheets, pillows, coverlets and ruffled bed skirts wait to welcome overnight guests. Granny Sue enters each room pulling back the drapes, letting in the early morning's sunlight smiling. She leaves one room and enters another repeating the same routine every day.

She expects the quiet will not last long. Soon her grandchildren will barge into the house, making such a ruckus, and reprimands will follow.

"They promised, this time they will come." She says so loud her voice echoes off the high ceiling hallway. Days, weeks, months and years pass. Granny Sue's ritual never waivers; the empty house once filled with joyful noise, children playing, sliding down the stair rail, laugher that filled this home is just memories of a time long past.

Now the years show decay---what was once shiny and well kept--- has cobwebs. The bed linens faded from the sun and threadbare give off an eerie ghostlike appearance... The stair rails are now dried and splintered.

The quiet wished for long ago is regretted; but she still hopes a promised visit will bring once more, a joyful noise.

ROCK CHRONICLES II: THE END
Shanda Whittle

Jimi and Pearl hiked through the eerie forest shrouded in fog atop Overlook Mountain. The spring sky was shadowed by heavy clouds suspended from the heavens. It was the heavens that ruled this land, filled with ruins from the past. Hidden at an elevation of 3,140 feet in the Catskill Mountains, tourists can look out over the site of where the Woodstock Music Festival took place in 1969, the defining moment of the 1960s counterculture.

"What is this place?" asked Pearl as she followed Jimi up to the ruins of a large building. There was a misty veil covering the crumbling brick walls and caved-in roof of what was once the Overlook Mountain House hotel.

The hotel was the centerpiece of a plan in the early 1800s to attract tourists to this rural New York area. The building was opened for business in1871. In 1873 President Ulysses S. Grant arrived, and history was made. It would be 96 years before history was made again in the upstate New York region.

"Welcome to my digs, sister!" Jimi exclaimed. A ghostly blanket of white was draped behind an aging wall showing the silhouette of what was once windows. Below the windows was a large open archway welcoming Jimi and Pearl forward. Stones in the walkway leading up to the wall were uprooted by decades of icy winters.

"None of this makes sense. I don't remember anything. We're old! What in the hell happened?" Janis desperately questioned, her temper starting to flare.

"Calm down, sister. I hate to tell you this, but you're dead! There's a Buddhist monk nearby I can take you too if you need help understanding that."

This peaceful enclave, several miles above Woodstock, New York, was also home to a utopian society in the early 1800s. ATibetan monastery was built atop the mountain in 1863 covering the area with a spiritual blanket. A Buddhist teacher from the monastery once said: "As long as there is life, there is pain and suffering" and "eventually people find in the Buddha's teaching there is a lot of remedy for how to get rid of pain and suffering, and how to apply happiness to their own lives."

"Do I look like I'm into the damn Buddha? I just want to know what the hell is going on! The last thing I remember was a big yellow taxi picking me up and bringing me here," she said, pushing her hair out of her face to take a better look around. She walked deeper into the aging hotel ruins, into an ocean of white mist. She felt the moist spring air hugging her and blinding her at the same time. Relying on touch and sound, she continued forward until she heard a sound.

She stopped and asked, "What was that?" She pushed her glasses further up her nose to see better, but they were fogged up by the mountain mist. She heard banging and rattling nearby as if someone was locked up and trying to break on through the mountain. Then she heard screams.

"Jimi?" She felt his hand on her elbow.

"I'm here. It's okay," Jimi said as he tried to figure out how to help her acclimate to her new 'life'. A thunderous shaking and rageful screams came from the direction of a darkened path outside the hotel. A flock of crows and a pair of gigantic vultures departed from a tree that was growing in the center of the hotel ruins. Janis screamed and jumped into Jimi's arms. Jimi held her with a slight grin on his face.

"I should have told you. We're not alone," he said, letting this sink in before telling her anything more.

"Wh-what do you mean we're not alone?" she asked cautiously as the screams continued to float toward them. He gently took her hand, knowing he had to be careful. She might have a heart attack if I tell her, he thought to himself.

"Why don't we take a walk. He's probably passed out by now," Jimi said.

"A walk where? Who's passed out? What is going on," she asked as her temper and fear began to boil over.

"I could tell you who, but you wouldn't believe me. C'mon, I promise it's nothing dangerous," he said, hold-ing his breath as he waited for her reaction.

"Nothing dangerous? Did you just hear the screams and rage I heard? Did you feel the earth shaking like I did? Not dangerous?" She spit out her words some-where between anger and terror. "Jimi. I'll ask you one more time. What do you mean we're not alone?"

He put his hand behind her waist and guided her down the dark path through the ruins. As they walked, he began to carefully give her enough information to ease her fears.

"This place is somewhat of a musician's graveyard," he began. "The skeleton of this hotel is what was left after three fires and a suicide in the span of 100 years. I guess you'd say this part of the mountain is haunted." He held his breath as he waited for her reaction. Then he heard it. A melody was floating from the back door. She stopped dead in her tracks.

"What's that? I recognize that song," she said as goose pimples rose across her body. She began to sway to the melody as her mind tried to remember the night she danced to it long ago. Then she heard it. His voice. She remembered his strung-out eyes, his disheveled hair, and his tight leather pants. Then came his voice.

"This is the end. Beautiful friend. This is the end. My only friend. The end."

Her jaw dropped, and she fell to the ground in awe. A plume of dust rose around her from the fall. Jimi let out a deep sigh and asked her, "Do you remember the lizard king?"

Sitting in awe, Janis remembered the night Jim Morrison pursued her. The night she had desires for him but rejected him because of his drunken, rude, and obnoxious behavior. Then there was the night Paul Rothchild tried to get Janis and Jim together thinking they would be the king and queen of rock-n-roll.

Her shock began to subside, and she began to laugh. It started as a soft giggle and turned into a full belly laugh. "Oh, Jim. By the sounds of things tonight, he hasn't changed much. Sounds like he's still a pain in the ass. Do you remember the night I knocked him out with a bottle of Southern Comfort? What a waste of good booze," she said with a look of reminiscence in her eyes, remembering the night she turned down Jim Morrison's advances. "He's here, too?" she asked.

"He's here," Jimi said. "Be nice to him. We have to get along here. People are strange, and Jim is a strange one. But he's one of us. Family. That's him at the back door. Man will try to move mountains before using his common sense.

"Welcome to the Morrison Hotel," Jimi told an awe-struck Janis. As they walked, they heard a calmer Jim Morrison reciting "Graveyard Poem":

It was the greatest night of my life
Although I still had not found a wife
I had my friends
Right there beside me
We were close together
We tripped the wall and we
Scaled the graveyard
Ancient shapes were all around us
The wet dew felt fresh beside the fog
Two made love in an ancient spot
One chased a rabbit in the dark

A girl got drunk and balled the dead
And I gave empty sermons to my head
Cemetery, cool and quiet
Hate to leave your sacred lay
Dread the milky coming of day (The Doors).

"Is he still reciting that stupid poem of his? Man, people are strange," Janis said with a grand smile on her face. She was home.

The Doors. (2007). Graveyard Poem." On Live in Boston. Los Angeles: Bright Midnight/Rhino Records (Recorded April 10, 1970).

ROYAL PALM BEACH WRITERS
AUTHORS

Hartley Barnes is a veteran who has served in three wars: Vietnam, Desert Storm, and Iraqi Freedom. Retiring from the U.S. Army in 2006, he went to work in Iraq and Afghanistan as a civilian contractor for six years. He now calls Florida his home and writes, focusing on creative literature and playwriting. Hartley is the Silver Medal Winner (2nd place) for the 2019 National Veterans Creative Arts Competition in writing organized by the Department of Veteran's Affairs.

Website: RoyalPalmBeachWriters.com/writers/hartley-barnes/
Email: Hartley@RoyalPalmBeachWriters.com
Website: HartleyBarnes.com

Margie Bonner was born and raised in Canada. Her professional career includes thirty years at JFK Hospital, working as a nurse. She considers the art of writing a true gift. For her, a novice writer, it is the joy of the journey. She is one of the original founders of the Writing Group of Royal Palm Beach. In addition, the pleasure she finds from her family, and the group gives Margie much joy and true satisfaction.

Website: RoyalPalmBeachWriters.com/writers/margie-bonner/
Email: Margie@RoyalPalmBeachWriters.com

Don Conway, Prof. Emeritus got hooked on story-telling and writing in 2012. The Veterans Administration awarded him a Gold Medal in 2014 and Gold and Silver Medals in 2015 for his entries in the VA's National Creative Arts Competition. The RPWG is his go-to family/support group.

Website: RoyalPalmBeachWriters.com/writers/don-conway/
Email: Don@RoyalPalmBeachWriters.com

Karina G. Felix was born and raised in Aruba. She's had a love for reading and a passion for writing since her early youth. She merged her passions for dance, metaphysical living, and writing into two magazine publications. She is the founder of Ingenious Publishers Inc. which is the publishing house for DANZ'N magazine, Lifestyle Living Magazine and Spectrum Volume 14 and 15.

Website: RoyalPalmBeachWriters.com/writers/karina-g-felix/
Email: Karina@RoyalPalmBeachWriters.com
Website: KarinaGFelix.com

Gloria Ferrara enjoys writing about times spent with family and friends she left moving to Florida in 1985. Through her stories, she renews experiences shared with them. She is one of the original founders of the Writing Group of Royal Palm Beach.

Website: RoyalPalmBeachWriters.com/writers/gloria-ferrara/
Email: Gloria@RoyalPalmBeachWriters.com

Virginia Guido is a retired NYC school administrator, living in Florida. She is married to Ralph, her childhood sweetheart, for 43 years. Her twin daughters (Natalie and Paulette) produced grandsons (Jax, Gio, and Jet) and a princess granddaughter (Bianca). Her son, Frankie, died in 2008. Virginia likes writing memoirs about her eccentric past. The Writing Group/Family is her therapeutic support.

Website: RoyalPalmBeachWriters.com/writers/virginia-guido/
Email: Virginia@RoyalPalmBeachWriters.com

Shelley Leiman has always been a creative soul but too modest to admit it. Her talents are; playing the piano, sewing costumes, devising treasure hunts for birthdays, baking pies, and even winning a radio jingle competition. Drama and writing rescued her when Shelley was widowed for the second time. An active member of a drama group, she considers herself a novice writer, currently working on her memoirs. Shelley has three children, five grandchildren, and degrees in sociology and special education. She lives in West Palm Beach.

Email: Shelley@RoyalPalmBeachWriters.com

Dorothy M. Littlefield is the author of Journey into the Land of the Wingless Giants, her first published novel. She enjoys writing humorous stories, romance, mysteries, and fairytales. She lived in Kilgore, Texas, and raised horses before she moved to West Palm Beach, Florida, to be near her daughter.

Website: RoyalPalmBeachWriters.com/writers/d-m-littlefield/
Email: Dorothy@RoyalPalmBeachWriters.com

Judith Ann Pelio was born and raised in New York City. She moved to Florida in 1991 after her twin sister became a Floridian. Judy has a Business Degree from New York University and a Master's Degree from the New

York Institute of Technology. She enjoys writing emotion-
ally-charged poetry, short stories, memoirs, and essays.
She is currently working on a book dedicated to and in
honor of her twin sister, Joanne, who passed away from a
malignant brain tumor.
Website: RoyalPalmBeachWriters.com/writers/judith-ann-pelio/
Email: Judith@RoyalPalmBeachWriters.com

John F. Rifenberg was born around Christmas, in
a shed near a barn. The barn was occupied by some
strangers from out of town. They got there first by don-
key, beating his parents to the barn. There were several people gathered around the manger in the barn. A
huge star in the north, brighten the night Then an angel,
named Frankie came from heavens or the highway, saved
the boy. As an older (but no wiser) man, he joined the
Royal Palm Beach Writers and helped re-invent the al-
phabet. By the grace of God, he has been rewarded with
five gold medals for his short stories in recent years.
Website: RoyalPalmBeachWriters.com/writers/john-rifenberg/
Email: John@RoyalPalmBeachWriters.com

Virginia (Ginny) Smythe is a recovering workahol-
ic that escaped corporate America. She moved to the
Acreage, Florida from Maryland eleven years ago and
has not looked back. Writing is her newest creative outlet, but she also has an entire room in her house dedicated to her sewing/embroidery hobby. She is a happy
go lucky kind of gal with a house full of dogs and plays a
serious game of poker.
Website: RoyalPalmBeachWriters.com/writers/virginia-smythe/
Email: Ginny@RoyalPalmBeachWriters.com

Patti Thomas grew up on the shores of Lake Superior in northern Wisconsin. Always active in music during her youth, she went on to become a music therapist and piano teacher. Her first love, though, has always centered around books: Reading, writing, and stockpiling them. Libraries are her favorite establishments.

Email: Patti@RoyalPalmBeachWriters.com

Tajuana Troy is currently a member of the Royal Palm Beach Writers Group. In her spare time, she enjoys reading, attending church, and walks on the beach. She and her family live a dedicated holistic vegan lifestyle for many years. She writes because it brings healing to her, and she believes it can help others.

Website: RoyalPalmBeachWriters.com/writers/tajuana-troy/
Email: Tajuana@RoyalPalmBeachWriters.com

Shanda Whittle is a Colorado/Georgia/and finally a Buffalo native who went to school in Maine to become a nurse. It's a long story. She is enjoying her snowless days here in Florida with the Royal Palm Beach Writers, where she successfully aspired towards her first-grade dream of becoming a book technician, AKA, a writer. She is the author of "Can't Find My Way Home: Memoir of a Wounded Healer", her first book.

Website: RoyalPalmBeachWriters.com/writers/shanda-whittle/
Email: Shanda@RoyalPalmBeachWriters.com

ROYAL PALM BEACH
WRITERS
ENCOURAGING ASPIRING WRITERS

===================================
PROGRAMS AND EVENTS
===================================-

Royal Palm Beach Writers invites you to enter their
ANNUAL WRITING CONTEST

Are you a poet in the making?
Love to write short stories?
Want to get published?
We are looking to inspire new writers!
===================================

Join us at our
MONTHLY OPEN MIC EVENT

We meet once a month at a local venue to read,
share, network and socialize with other writers.
===================================

BECOME A MEMBER

Our group meets twice a month to hone our writing skills
and offer constructive critique that helps each member
improve in their writing skills set and thought process.

Request more information:
Info@RoyalPalmBeachWriters.com
===================================

ORDER NOW!
You can order previously
published copies of Spectrum here:
Spectrum@RoyalPalmBeachWriters.com
===================================

FIND US
Follow us on Social Media:
Facebook: https://www.facebook.com/groups/RPBWgroup/
Instagram: https://www.instagram.com/royalpalmbeachwriters/
Website: https://www.RoyalPalmBeachWriters.com/